I0719015

Felix Publishing 2022
email: info.felixpublishing@gmail.com
Print copies available from publisher.

Orion and Other Stories of the Future

Print Edition ISBN: 978-1-925662-46-7
Digital Edition ISBN: 978-1-925662-47-4

Author: Dr Peter T. Scott

Registration:
Thorpe-Bowker +61 3 8517 8342
email: bowkerlink@thorpe.com.au

This is a work of fiction. The characters in this book did not exist and the politics of the time have been generalized. No disrespect is meant to any person living or dead.

Orion

and
Other Stories
of the Future

Peter T. Scott

First released 2022

Table of Contents

ORION

1.

The enormous road train trundled down the last stretch of the winding Great Western Highway which came steeply down through the sandstone cliffs off the slopes of Mount Victoria. Soon the huge Double-B semi-trailer would be out onto the great plains which extended without much relief across the western part of the state. The sound of the free-wheeling electric motors now involved in regenerative braking echoed through the deep sandstone cuttings.

The sandstone cliffs which marked the western edge of the Blue Mountains were now bathed in the red glow of the setting sun with only the deeper valleys being shadowed by the dark blue haze for which these mountains were famous. It had been a long and slow haul up from the coastal strip on the other side of the mountains which formed part of the Great Dividing Range which ran down most of the eastern part of Australia for over 3500 kilometres. The road train with its thirty-six wheels, sixteen of which were driven by powerful Siemens DC electric motors, needed all of their combined power of 600 kilowatts to crawl up the giant Lapstone Monocline. The long-nose of the prime mover contained the monstrous diesel-electric generating system needed for such power as well as eight of the main driving axles and their individual motors.

Now, as the sun shone its long, faint fingers across the darkening plain below, the driver relaxed and changed channels on his radio to get some of the western music he played on his long trips between Sydney and Wagga Wagga some 400 kilometres down the A41.

"Ya don't mind a bit o' music, do ya mate" he said to his passenger. It was probably a waste of time asking such a question as the big man in black sitting in the passenger's seat had not said a word since leaving their depot in Parramatta in the western suburbs of the city. The driver thought that he was a hard man but the man sitting in the passenger's seat was in a higher league; big, large scarred hands and a face which looked like it was blasted out of hard granite. Given the driver's cheery "all aboard", the man in black had simply given him a stern frown and replied, "Just drive. I'll tell you when to stop".

Passengers were not often taken on these trips; usually only company personnel going from one depot to another. Earlier that day, the dispatcher had told the driver, more as a caution than anything, that he would have a passenger for part of his trip. He was one of the Boss's Special Projects Division boys; a shadowy group of hard individuals who appeared occasionally at depots and other places to handle some of the more difficult tasks that often occurred in the trucking industry. Drivers and those desk-wallahs in administration only talked in hushed tones about the boys of the SPD. They had been used very publicly in some of violent altercations with the powerful Transport Workers' Union back in the '30s but things had been quiet over the last few years. No doubt the Boss had seen to that.

Rex Transport, the company which the driver had worked for more than ten years was owned entirely by Con Vassiliadis whom everyone called the Boss. Con had been the typical Greek boy whose grandparents had immigrated from the 'old country' in the 1950s and whose parents saw to it that young Con had the best that they could afford. Distaining a long education, the young man had taken to driving for a now extinct trucking company. A few years of hard work and Con Vassiliadis had purchased his first semi-trailer which he used across the interstate road network to deliver the more risky items of cargo. This eventually earned him enough money to buy several more trucks and set up his now extensive haulage company. Rex Transport he called it; a play on his name which referred to those things owned by a king which he then Latinised to Rex which had the same meaning.

Con Vassiliadis was a hard man who made sure that his employees worked hard for their low salaries. He was not like most of his Greek Australians who generally were open, fair-minded and gregarious. Con Vassiliadis was driven by ambition, he kept his plans to himself, rarely discussing them with his family. He could be friendly and generous when it suited him and he had many friends, if one could call them that, in big business and the government, irrespective of which party was in power.

After the introduction of the Fossil Fuel Act in 2040, driven by pressure from the Green Party on a weak government, most of the large haulage companies went to the wall and left the carrying of long-distance freight to the poorly-resourced government rail systems. With the withdrawal of fossil fuels from the open market, many of these companies had downsized their operations and now used smaller, electrically-powered commuter trucks to carry goods on the short-haul routes between rail termini and their city depots. Not so Rex Transport. The Boss and seen this coming, with some help from his friends in the government, and had bought up as many diesel storage farms as he could get. Naturally these had been cheap to purchase, even with a full supply of the fuel. It did not take much persuasion and some considerable amount of unrecorded cash 'donations' to certain members of parliament to secure a 'special consideration' in using diesel-electric road trains which naturally would be 'in the country's defence interest'. The rest of the transport business considered the Boss a dangerous man to deal with and something of a reactionary. With a rare trace of humour, or simply just dark cynicism, the Boss introduced a snarling tyrannosaurus rex as the logo for his company before having it painted on all of his trucks.

Back on the road, the driver was happy and confident as he had done this run many times. Pick up the rig from the depot and drive the six hours to the other depot at Wagga Wagga. Most of the trip would be at night and it would be late by the time he reached the country depot. A few beers in the local Soldiers Club and then a good night's sleep ready to pick up a north-bound rig the next morning and back along the same route to home base; his current load would be taken on further south and then west to a mine site in the furthest corner of the state.

The road train had now turned south along route A41 as the driver turned on the bank of big spotlights on the front of the rig. There was hardly any traffic on the road as Rex Transport had the monopoly on long distance haulage, thanks to more 'lobbying' by the Boss. Private cars and small trucks usually did not venture out onto the highway these days as the oil companies had been slow in replacing their service stations with charging stations. Having a dead battery late at night was not much of an option for the private traveller. Not much of a chance for that to happen with the big road train as it usually carried enough diesel to get between depots and there also was a bank of backup lithium batteries behind the spacious cab. If a careless driver had forgotten to top up his fuel on a really long haul, then these batteries would make up the distance, albeit at a much-reduced speed.

The passenger leaned over and took an electronic device the size of a cell phone from the backpack which sat between his legs on the cabin floor. The driver took a quick glance at it when the screen lit up. It was a hand-held GPS device.

"Three more kilometres until we stop." The passenger said in a firm voice which startled the driver out of his concentration looking out along the beams of the spotlights for any kangaroos which would suddenly decide to bound out of the close scrub and into the path of the road train.

"O.K," was the only reply that the driver felt that was needed to his taciturn passenger as he looked down at the odometer on the dashboard and noted its last few digits. He would be glad to rid himself of this passenger; no joy and distraction from the tedious routine of driving from this hard character.

A few moments later, the passenger raised a gloved hand and pointed to a sign on the side of the road which read Rest Stop 100 metres.

"Pull in here, driver. I will expect you back here on your return trip." The passenger said, pulling his backpack up from the floor of the cab.

The driver did as he was told and pulled the big road train into the rest stop. Without any further conversation, the passenger opened the cab door and climbed out into the darkness, slamming the door behind him.

"And goodbye to you! Looking forward to seeing you again. Not!" the driver thought as he put the road train in gear and moved back onto the highway. Why he would stop in this remote spot was beyond his comprehension. There was nothing anywhere near here except the old Air Force base which had been sold off years ago.

The passenger waited until the rear lights of the road train disappeared around the next bend before quickly crossing the deserted road. There was no moon tonight, a consideration which had been in his planning, and so he unstrapped his backpack and brought out a pair of night vision goggles which he strapped around his head. They were the latest Generation 5, AN/PVS unit which gave a very sharp albeit a fine-grained monochrome image of a grey-green colour. Using this headset, he could now easily navigate through the thick eucalypt scrub which lined both sides of the road. His destination was only a few kilometres away, he confirmed, as he quickly took a bearing from his small GPS unit.

The going was not difficult as the land around here consisted of the low, rolling hills of the western plains. Most of it had been cleared in the early days when the first settlers were able to cross the Blue Mountains in the 1820's. Only the creeks and the roads and a few patches of less arable land now stood under the old eucalypt forest.

It was the best part of an hour before he finally reached his destination. He carefully walked up a small gully leading up to the plain beyond, slowly feeling for dead twigs and hollows in the ground; a natural habit he had got into after many years as a Forward Scout in the Asian War.

His night vision goggles easily picked out the high cyclone wire fence with its grotesque topping of razor wire but there was something else. A long, red beam of LASER light ran a few centimetres above the ground parallel to the fence. "No problems," he thought as the beam was inside the fence perimeter. His mission this time did not require a breach of the perimeter fence, only its security.

He found a small grassy knoll just outside of the fence which gave a clear view of the grassy field which stretched out to the limits of his goggles' range. Now he needed something a bit more sophisticated. He had found through bitter experience that the monocular night vision goggles, even of the best quality, were useful in moving through the country, but it required the additional power of true night vision binocular to make an appraisal of the countryside over distance. Replacing his goggles into his backpack, he then pulled out his Night Owl NOB8X Generation 4 binoculars before settling down into a comfortable prone position to search the countryside on the other side of the wire fence.

He scanned slowly from left at the tree line to past the group of buildings which were directly in front to his extreme right, back at the tree line. No security posts except the occasional and expected television cameras mounted on poles just inside the fence line, directed along its length in both directions. No doubt they would also have infra-red capabilities but he was well out of their range here low to the ground on the other side of the fence.

He shifted his view back to the buildings which consisted of one three-story main structure, which was obviously old barracks and administration, and several small buildings set away from it. The rest of the countryside beyond was open and flat as would be expected from a former Air Force base. He fingered the magnification knob which enabled him to zoom into the main building itself. Third floor, fourth window from the right had been the intelligence received by the SPD from their man inside this facility.

There it was. The window was open and there was just a faint glow of light within. He put his binoculars down and reached into the main compartment of the backpack to retrieve a small tripod, an infra-red gunsight and another device which was about the size of a bulky laptop but with the barrel of a lens protruding from its bulbous top. The unit was complete when he unfolded a large hollow dish antenna which opened up like some giant silver three-dimensional fan. He positioned this reflector, for that was the purpose of the box-like structure, so that its opened side would face towards the main building. He secured the gun sight onto its mounting on top of the reflector and sighted through it so that it was directly facing the window in the main building beyond.

This installed device was the latest in Free Space Optical (FSO) communications systems which could send a pre-coded message along a narrow frequency LASER beam to a similar device over a considerable distance. Tonight, he expected to obtain and download all of the data and latest work details of the secret project now being constructed within the old base. It would only take a second or two to download this information sent along the LASER beam from a corresponding unit in the main building.

He pressed the small button on his wrist watch which illuminated the dial with a faint green glow showing that he still had fifteen minutes before the appointed time for the transmission at 2130 hours. Everything had been checked before he left base but he switched on the unit, making sure that there was no visible light, only a small glow from the gunsight. There was nothing now but to wait for the appointed time which he did with his usual patience.

Time passed slowly as it does in all such waiting situations and now it was time to receive the transmission, but first, he would have to signal his contact that all was ready. This was done using a small LASER penlight which he took from his top pocket and gave three on-off signals towards the open window. There was the same signal repeated from the darkened room of the building. Everything was now ready for the quick LASER signal carrying the encoded message to be transferred between the two devices and then his work for the night was done.

Suddenly, the light in the room on the third floor, fourth from the right came on. He quickly snatched up his binoculars and reset them to normal mode and looked towards the light. There was movement within the room. At least two men. The faint sound of a gunshot echoed though the still night air. His contact had been discovered and soon he would expect a security patrol to be searching this very patch of bush.

He quickly dismantled the communication device and replaced his night vision goggles. Ensuring that every item was secured in the backpack, he carefully rearranged the leaves and twigs where he was lying and carefully retreated down the gully towards the distant highway. He would cross this and find a secure, well-camouflaged place further back in the forest until the next day in the hope that he could then make his planned rendezvous with the road train on its return journey back to his base in the city.

He hoped that any security search did not go much
past the perimeter fence of the secret establishment.

2.

The sound of the gunshot seemed to be extremely loud in the small storeroom where the gun was fired. It echoed down the corridor of the main building and in the boardroom just a few doors down, it stopped Sir Ewan Hunter, CEO of Project Orion in mid-sentence.

"What the devil was that?" he said, jumping up from the end of the conference table.

"It sounded like a gunshot!" replied Ted Campbell, the projects Chief Engineer who sat further down the table and who now also stood up. Both men rushed to the door and went out into the darkened corridor. There was a light coming from the small storeroom further down from the boardroom. Sir Ewan was not a man to hold back in any situation and so he strode purposely down to the light. What he saw in the storeroom was another shock. On the floor was a body, now being turned over by the head of security, Troy Jaeger who knelt beside it, his SIG Sauer P365 pistol in his hand. He now looked up at the group of men crowding the doorway.

"Sorry about the noise, Sir Ewan, but I think that I've found our saboteur." he said, getting to his feet. Jaeger was a large man; well over six feet and with an athletic build. He had been recruited from the Australian SAS when he had resigned his commission as Captain. A forelock of his black hair partly fell over his craggy face and his smile and laconic way of speaking often jarred with Sir Ewan's need for detail. He walked over to the doorway and pulled a small, flat, double-sided throwing knife from the doorjamb.

"Who was it?

"Jim Dawson"

"One of your men?" Sir Ewan looked up from the body with a frown on his round face.

"A good one too – a former mercenary from South Africa and a hard man. But it looks like he had a better offer." Jaeger said turning to the black electronic apparatus sitting on a low table near the open window. "A LASER communication device. I caught him getting ready to send a signal to someone outside the facility. If you don't mind, Sir Ewan, I'll get my team out to search the perimeter."

"Yes…yes…of course, Jaeger. But what about the late Mr Dawson?"

Jaeger turned to his superior and shook his head. "Don't worry, Sir Ewan. He's not going anywhere and I'll send some men to clean up this mess after we search the grounds but the body has to remain here until the police arrive. Might I request that you contact the station at Bathurst – the Sargent there is a particular friend of mine and he will keep this quiet."

"Yes, thank you, Jaeger. We don't want the snoops from Sydney running all over the place with the launch tomorrow."

He quietly closed the storeroom door and its bloody occupant as Jaeger left and turned to the others who had gathered in the corridor eager to find out what had happened. "Well, ladies and gentlemen, it looks like the conference is over for now. Please return to your rooms and we will try to sort out the details for the launch in the morning."

Dr. Paul Sinclair, the project's scientific advisor followed the rest of the group down the stairwell to the ground floor. He noted that the security floodlights were already coming on along the wire mesh fence along the distant tree line. What a mess! He thought. He did not like Jaeger but he had to acknowledge that he was good at his job, but he was ex-bloody-SAS and too suave for his liking. Sinclair was a quiet academic who had got to his position in Project Orion through his intelligence and knowledge of electrical systems. He had spent most of his early life at school and university being the target of such men. He hated that type of cocky individual. He felt that this feeling of antagonism towards Jaeger was mutual. Jaeger was not an easy man to like unless one was female and preferred the rugged type. Well, tomorrow is another day and there were a few issues which he would have to take up with Ted Campbell the engineer about the voltage capacity of the new lithium-tungsten batteries.

The next morning came slowly. Many of the staff at Project Orion seemed rather jaded at the long breakfast table in the old Air Force Mess. It had been a rough night for most of the staff, especially those who had been at the late-night conference and witnessed the results of the shooting. The others had heard about the event either later that night or earlier that morning. Everyone was in some state of confusion or apprehension. Only Jaeger who had seen more bodies than he would care to remember and Sir Ewan Campbell who seemed to be able to put aside such events, were able to eat a substantial breakfast.

There had been an extensive security search of the perimeter of the old Air Force base both later that night and in the early morning. The small electric all-terrane vehicles generally used around the base had followed the perimeter fence in its entirety and all of the data from the security cameras had been checked pixel by pixel. Security teams of two men each had also patrolled outside the perimeter fence, especially between it and the A41 highway to the east. Nothing had been found and the highway was deserted as expected except for a lone road-train disappearing over a distant hill on its north-bound route to Sydney. That team thought nothing of this as it was a regular route and usual time for the big road-train to pass by. Nothing unusual.

The Bathurst police had arrived early that morning and had the body removed from the storeroom after a thorough search. Jaeger had explained that he had seen door of the storeroom ajar and had entered and switched on the light. Dawson at the LASER device had been startled and had pulled a knife from his boot and had thrown it at Jaeger. Jaeger's trained response was to shoot his assailant. Self-defence was the immediate impression of the investigating Police.

The electronic gear which had been used for transferring the secrets of the Project Orion had also been removed by Jaeger who needed to find out just how much data had been sent. Sargent Quinlan from the police, who knew Jaeger from his early security checks on the personnel of Project Orion, had accepted his story of self-defence, especially when Jaeger handed over the throwing knife and pointed out the cut in the doorjamb.

Sir Ewan had telephoned the Sargent's superior at Bathurst Station and had been reassured that the Media would be kept out of the investigation until well after the launch of Project Orion. This was more than acceptable to Sir Ewan who always believed that even such unpleasant connections between the project and Dawson's death would still be good publicity.

At breakfast in the big former mess hall, Sir Ewan stood up and gave a brief account of the previous night's events and possible problems which may be encountered should the story be leaked to the Media. All cell phone conversations were then forbidden until after the launch of the project and he made it clear than any disregard of his wishes would mean instant dismissal. There was, naturally the usual buzz of excited conversation after he had left the table, but then one by one and in small groups the assembled staff went back to their work in making Project Orion ready for its grand launch the next day. Meanwhile, the old base had been locked down by Jaeger's security team and no on-base personnel were permitted to leave. There were no scheduled deliveries of goods, and the only expected visitors were the representative from the Chinese Jīn Tàiyáng Engineering Company of Jiangsu and the invited guests later that evening.

About midday, Sir Ewan Hunter called Jaeger into his office and quietly shut the door. He walked over to his desk and clicked on the intercom button to instruct his private secretary, Mrs. Scanlon, to hold any calls and visitors. He moved to behind his desk and motioned Jaeger to also sit down on the chair which he had positioned in the centre of the room.

"So, Jaeger! Last night was a bit of a cock up, what?" his early life in the slums of Glasgow starting to appear in his usually urbane, educated voice. "But no matter. I am convinced, and so are the police, that you had little choice in the matter. What exactly was Dawson doing in the storeroom?"

Jaeger settled himself more comfortably in the chair and looked up at Sir Ewan.

"Well now, he had rather a sophisticated LASER communication system which could have been used to send considerable pre-recorded data along a beam to a receiver in a few seconds. A great device in combat situations where radio signals could be easily monitored. Dawson would have known that we had just such radio monitoring and other surveillance equipment and so he obviously smuggled this particular unit in and hid it in the storeroom. We keep a lot of electronic equipment there and so it would have been overlooked during our usual checks."

"And who do you think was at the other end of this LASER beam? Sir Ewan enquired with leaning across the table.

"Your guess is as good as mine, sir" Jaeger replied, his outstretch hands and a rather vacant look did not really answer his superior's question. "But you have a lot of enemies who are suspicious that you are up to something monumental in the long-distance travel department."

"Unfortunately, too true, Jaeger. I haven't been in the long-haul aviation business these many years without some of my competitors being rather paranoid, especially those of Greek extraction, if you know what I mean."

"Rex Transport you mean sir?" there was silence for a few seconds and Sir Ewan rustled a few papers on his desk trying to avoid any direct accusations. Jaeger continued:

"I hardly think that that old dinosaur would go to such trouble. He already has a monopoly on road transport which even the rail system cannot match."

"True, Jaeger. But he has a lot of powerful people, even some of those coming tonight, behind him and he is the sort of man who hates to be beaten. I know. I have met him several times and he is one hard customer who would stop at nothing to prevent

Project Orion from going ahead. And this is what we must now talk about!"

Jaeger moved uncomfortably in his chair. Sir Ewan Hunter had a similar reputation, both as a hard man and how he did business, to Con Vassiliadis. Both were self-made billionaires who had started with nothing.

"Do you really think that the unfortunate Dawson was our saboteur? In the few occasions which I had dealings with him he seemed to be just a competent security guard with more years on him than most and nothing much else. Some of our acts of sabotage showed some distinct intelligence and understanding of the damage that would be caused."

"Perhaps you are right, Sir Ewan, but Jim Dawson's military record was impressive even for an older man. He had considerable experience as a mercenary in southwestern Africa and was an expert in the use of sophisticated weapons."

"Never-the-less, Jaeger. I am not convinced that he was the only saboteur within our organisation. You may remember the fire in the oil shed way back in the early days of the project. That was before you hired Dawson. Is that correct?

"Yes, sir. Dawson was hired at the end of our first year when the size of the project was getting beyond that of my small team. That fire in the oil shed was put down as spontaneous combustion and we instituted a set of SOPs to reduce flammable wastes in and around that area."

"Possibly. But I cannot afford any more 'events,' shall we say, with our launch imminent. So! Let us assume that we have at least one additional saboteur in our midst. Someone who knows what they are about and how the project operates. So, who is he…or even she? And what is their motive"

Jaeger stood up and walked slowly over to the front of Sir Ewan's desk then turned and walked back again, his mind now lost apparently in thought.

"Well, sir. Let's assume that everyone here is a potential saboteur and that they have a motive for seeing the demise of this project." Jaeger walked over to the long magnetic whiteboard on the wall behind where Sir Ewan was sitting.

"Let me list the people who have both the intelligence and capability of doing some damage." He picked up a whiteboard marker and began to write on the board whilst he spoke.

"At the bottom of our list are the many tradesmen and women involved in construction. Like Dawson, they could have the ability and outside support with the main motive being a sizeable cash payment. Possible but not too likely. Dawson had those additional skills to do the job thoroughly.

Of our Executive Staff, we have some possibilities but most of them have been with you for years. Am I correct?"

"Alright, alright, Jaeger. Let's not go through the entire staff of Hunter Aviation!

Jaeger continued by writing the names of several senior members of Project Orion on the whiteboard.

"Firstly, there is your 2IC and Chief Engineer Edward Campbell. A good man and a very innovative engineer, but he has a high opinion of himself and grumbles a lot about not being paid to his ability. Perhaps some deep resentment there?"

"Balderdash! Ted Campbell has been a good friend and senior engineer at Hunter Aviation for many years. Of course, he grumbles about his salary! He's a fellow Scot! No, I don't think Ted would do any damage to this project. He is as passionate about it as I am. Next?"

"Next we have Dr. Paul Sinclair, your tame scientist."

"You don't seem to have hit it off with him, have you?" Sir Ewan said, giving Jaeger a sideways glance.

"Not really. You know the old saying that 'clever people are not to be trusted – like lawyers and grocers they weigh everything'. But that being just an intuition, I did notice when I did the background checks on all of the senior people here, that Sinclair was denied your support for a very prestigious scholarship to an American university. Perhaps he holds a grudge against you and this is his way of getting back."

"Nonsense! I went over that matter with Paul and I explained why I did not support his application. Firstly, the scholarship was only for a year and it was offered because the university was trying to establish a new department for their own glory. Secondly, I made it quite clear that his research and advice was much more important to my organisation and that I could not afford to let him go. Next!"

"Mr. Zhan Yisheng, who has just only recently and most conveniently arrived but who has been in and out of the base several times over the last two years. You know that his parent company, Jīn Tàiyáng Engineering has close relationships with the Communist government and his brother is the local Party Member in Jiangsu? The Chinese have their own version of project Orion and they don't like competition."

"Mr. Zhan has been indispensable in the construction side of Project Orion since its inception. Considering his background, which I myself checked on my recent visit to China, I would be surprised if he did not have connections with their government. No, I think that Mr Zhan is quite sincere about his specialised version of engineering and with his countrymen watching our work closely, he would 'lose face' if our project and his specific technology failed. So that about covers my immediate senior staff. Do you have any more suggestions?"

Jaeger walked over to Sir Ewan's desk and looked down at his superior and gave a wry smile."

"Well, if you want a complete security analysis and aren't afraid of complete honesty, we must also consider your motives, Sir Ewan."

"What do you mean?" he said, jumping to his feet and looking at the security chief directly. Sir Ewan was much shorter than Jaeger in height but just as broad. He had been brought up in the tough street gangs of his native Glasgow and was not afraid of confrontation.

Jaeger took a step backwards and shrugged his shoulders. "Well, you have a lot of Hunter Aviation invested in this single project. I'm only involved in security, not finances. I can only assume that this project is heavily insured and that your financial backers demand some sort of deadline for its completion. If there are some design faults which naturally would cause Project Orion to fail, some assistance for that to happen might get you some returns through a massive insurance payout."

"Look Jaeger, I pay you a great deal of money to look after my security here. Not to insult my intelligence and delve into matters beyond your comprehension. Remember that! And what about yourself now? Are you beyond suspicion?"

"To be honest – no!" But as you said, you pay me a great deal of money and Project Orion has been an easy job until now. Dawson's actions have shown that there are some big players out there who wish Project Orion to fail. That makes my security tasks here a mite more challenging but not beyond my capabilities. Dawson got through my background checks but I am happy about the rest of my team. They are just as annoyed and disappointed that one of our own should be up to no good. You can rest assured that no more little acts of sabotage will occur. I am sorry if I offended you, Sir Ewan, but honesty is the best policy when it comes to security."

Sir Ewan sat down and nervously straightened his desk papers for a second time. After a short period of silence, he looked up and Jaeger and gave a depreciating smile.

"Of course, Troy. I'm sorry. I wanted a security analysis and you gave me more than I expected. I still have that old Scottish fey that there may be more attempts on Project Orion and I rely on you to keep them from occurring. Keep your team on full alert and watch everyone." He stood up again and put out his hand. " Including me. O.K.?"

Jaeger took Sir Ewan's hand "Thank you Sir Ewan, you can rely on me." And turned and left the room.

Later that evening, the official guests started to arrive. Most had taken the electrified rail to Bathurst where they changed for a company electric commuter bus which took them to the main entrance to the old base and its mandatory security checks by Jaeger's staff. It then meant a long walk up to the main building but the expanse of the airfield, the buildings and their many floodlights as well as the cold air only added to their interest. A few of the wealthier guests came in personal transport ranging from the more powerful EVs to a small fixed and rotary wing electric aircraft. All guests were checked thoroughly through surveillance gates before being personally escorted into the old Mess Hall in the main building which had been redecorated as a conference venue. Drinks and hors d'oeuvres were served by additional Hunter Aviation hostesses as the arriving guests entered. Most of the conversation centred around the mysterious Project Orion and why they had been personally invited. Many of the guests represented some of the international media networks although it had been stressed on the invitations that no cameras were allowed. Moreover, as each guest arrived and went through the x-ray surveillance gates, their cell phones were confiscated and tagged for later return. There was now a complete communication blackout with Project Orion and the outside world.

At exactly 1800 hours, Julie Wright, the projects PR Director walked into the room and announced over her microphone that the meeting would now start and that guests should take their numbered seats. She was tall, blonde and shapely, features that Jaeger had noticed on her arrival many months ago but she was also very intelligent and seemed to be impervious to his charms.

She gave a highly polished welcome, making the guests feel more at ease as was fitting her two Masters' Degree in Psychology and Sociology. A few subtle humorous references to some of the politicians and more important media personalities in the room put everyone into a receptive mood. She then introduced Head of Security Jaeger with a smile which was quickly extinguished as she left the podium.

Jaeger was also an old hand at handling a crowd, although he was more at ease with a company of troops. An apology of sorts was given about the confiscation of cell phones and the few cameras which some of the more determined of the media had tried to smuggle in. It was the next piece of information which made the audience sit up give gasps of annoyance or disbelief.

"I am sorry about the strict security, ladies and gentlemen, but there is a strong need for it as you will see later. We have had to put a complete veil of secrecy over the project since its inception as there are too many antagonistic forces and powerful people who would like to see this project fail. I hope you find your stay at Project Orion most exciting and we have a very interesting time ahead of us."

Jaeger paused for a moment and looked up at some of his now uniformed security team who were standing at the rear of the mess hall. He continued.

"Unfortunately, there is one other matter. Because of the tight security, once we reveal the true nature of

Project Orion, we must insist that you stay as our guests overnight and be part of our official project launch tomorrow morning. This was mentioned on the invitations and you were asked to make appropriate arrangements. If any of you now regret that you cannot be our guests, then I will have to ask you now to leave. Members of my team will escort you to your vehicles or take you to Bathurst where you can make other arrangements."

There was a murmur throughout the audience and several looked around to see who would stand up to leave. No one did.

"Good! Thank you, ladies and gentlemen, for your trust in our arrangements. I will now hand you back to Ms. Wright who will explain the rest of the nights proceedings."

Julie Wright came back to the microphone and gave her usual smile of reassurance.

"Well now! That was the bad news! Now the good. Soon we will reveal the secret of Project Orion by inviting you to come out to our main facility and see it for yourself. We will meet again and get some of the details about the project from our senior staff;

something of which I am sure some of the more technically-minded members of the media will have considerable interest. For those of you who are more interested in the future financial prospects, Sir Ewan Hunter, our CEO will discuss such issues over a very sumptuous dinner we have planned for you later this evening and then we offer you a good night's sleep before your participation in the launch of Project Orion tomorrow morning"

There was a pause as she made a dramatized sweep of her slender arm around the large Mess Hall.

"Oh! For those who have some knowledge of the previous function of this base, please be assured that there has been a complete renovation of the old barracks and that you will experience 5-star accommodation and food. No ten-by-ten wooden rooms with old lino and steel lockers and ration packs for guests of Hunter Aviation!"

This little touch of humour caused a ripple of laughter to go through the audience who now seemed to be in a good mood and looking forward to the rest of the night.

"Well, now! Thank you again ladies and gentlemen for your patience – and I might say your trust in Project Orion. You will see our team leaders in their bright blue jackets standing next to the several exits on our right. There is no hurry, so if you would like to leave your personal gear on your seats, we ask you now to go to the nearest door where your team leader will take you out to view the mysterious Project Orion. Good evening."

3.

"Wow! It's an airship!" came the exclamation from a young reporter from the *Herald* who had just passed through the double door which was set in the wall of a huge hanger just a short walk from the administration building.

The rest of his group bunched up as those who had entered first stopped in their tracks to take in the enormity of the building and the huge construction which it housed. The other groups came through similar doors along the side of the hanger with the noise of their hubbub echoing through the building. Gasps of awe and excitement went through all of those who had just entered.

"Come this way, ladies and gentlemen." said Sir Ewan Hunter over the loudspeakers position above the doorways. He was standing high up on a set of aircraft boarding stairs which were still further down the hanger. "Welcome to the *Orion*, Hunter Aviation's latest – and should I say – greatest new innovation. If you would care to follow your designated group leaders past my exalted position, you will find the main boarding stairs further down her hull. I invite you all aboard."

With that, he quickly dismounted the boarding stairs before walking smartly under and along the giant white hull of the airship and under the short stubby wing which protruded from its side. The more observant of the crowd which had now fully entered the hanger, noticed that the lower hull was indeed an extremely reflective white which ended about halfway up where it became an iridescent metallic dark blue.

At the main boarding stairs, which were broad and similar to a wide staircase, stood a smiling Julie Wright, the projects PR director.

"Welcome to the *Orion*, Ladies and Gentlemen." she said in a loud but friendly voice. "Your leaders will now take you aboard and get you seated. Have no fear, the *Orion* is quite stable and you will be safe as you would be in any convention centre."

A few of the guests held back, still in awe of the gigantic white hull under which they now stood, but most were enthusiastic to find out more about the airship and so followed their group leaders up the wide set of boarding stairs.

At the top of the stairs was a small corridor, much like that found when entering the main deck of a cruise ship. There were the usual baggage inspection machines with their long rollers to carry luggage through them and two personal x-ray portals to screen the passengers. These now were unattended, as all of the guests and their luggage had been inspected by Jaeger's security team earlier that evening. Past the security gates, the corridor turned sharply to the left and divided out into two separate corridors much like those found past the entrance doors of airliners. Guests were directed through these corridors by hostesses dressed in the Hunter Aviation uniform of light blue. They were again surprised by coming out into a wide cabin, very much like that of the interior of an old wide-bodied jet airliner but far broader. The cabin was indeed the size of a large convention room and was filled with many rows of aircraft passenger seats, four across separated by wide aisles carpeted in dark blue.

The group leaders led their awe-struck people down these aisles to the spacious front of the cabin where they were directed to sit in the centre front few rows of seats. This area was more like that of a convention centre rather than the sudden, cramped space behind some forward bulkhead of an aircraft. The wall in front of the seats was set back about ten metres, housing large television screens which were positioned along its length so that they faced each bank of seats. Those guests looking around the large, almost square cabin noticed that the side walls had portholes identical to those on aircraft but currently with their shutters closed. The level of excited conversation came to a crescendo filling the cabin as the guests turned this way and that to look around at the large, auditorium-like cabin.

The noise quickly subsided as Sir Ewan Hunter and his staff walked down the wide central aisle. Sir Ewan moved over to the small lectern which had been position in the front centre of the cabin and adjusted the microphone.

"Well, now my friends. Here we are! Finally, inside the Flight Cabin of the Airship *Orion*. Not quite like being inside of an aircraft's cabin and nor quite like sitting in an ocean liner's theatre, is it? And that just about puts the *Orion's* purpose into perspective. Please settle back into your chairs – luckily at this meeting you will not have to buckle up your seat belts." he said with a smile. "That will come tomorrow for those of you who wish to be part of our launch and demonstration cruise."

There were the turning of heads and more excited conversation as the guests took in what Sir Ewan had just said. 'Demonstration cruise' was the oft repeated term.

"Yes, friends. Tomorrow morning you will have a chance to come with us up into the silence of the clouds as we take the *Orion* up on its first official flight." Sir Ewan said using his hands to indicate silence. "We have called our airship the *Orion* for a number of reasons: firstly because it is designed to fly under that brilliant constellation of stars which shine so brightly in both the Southern and Northern Hemispheres; secondly, like the ancient Greek myth where Orion himself was the greatest of hunters, we shall be pursuing markets to transport stores and equipment to and from remote areas such as mining camps as well as people like yourselves in long haul passenger transport; and lastly – and I hope you will forgive a little bit of vanity – the name also alludes to my family's name."

A small ripple of good-natured humour went through the audience as Sir Ewan continued:

"Of course, we have been testing her for some time and I can assure you that like the old Scottish joke about what is worn under the kilt, everything is in perfect working order."

There was a short ripple of laughter from the audience.

"So now sit back and relax. The hostesses will soon be bringing along some food and drink – Gold Business Class, of course – whilst we tell you more about the *Orion*. You may take notes if you wish but a full package of information with technical specifications and some media videos will be handed out at the end of our presentation. You may use these items when you return to your companies copyright free."

Sir Ewan turned to Julie Wright to confirm that these were in fact ready then returned to the audience and said with a wry smile.

"Naturally, there will be no compulsion for any of you to go on our flight just in case any of you have reservations about flying. But I can assure you that it will be a great experience and nothing like any flight which you have experienced beforehand. Before I introduce you to each member of my technical department, let me outline briefly the advantages and potential uses of our airship – I am sure that you financial people would like to see the profits in our venture." he said with another enigmatic smile. He continued:

"The *Orion* has the great potential of doing many things which are costly and generally difficult to do in an age without fossil fuels and therefore limited transportation. Even my hydrogen-powered airlines cannot sustain the cargo-carrying capacity as they once did with avgas fuel. Nor can they just go anywhere they like. Rotary wing aircraft such as the larger drones simply do not have the lifting power for industrial cargos. So, let me quickly outline our advantages and possible uses." Sir Ewan turned towards the screen behind him on the wall and held up a handset. The screen became active with a list of possible uses for the *Orion*. They included:

1. Advanced, passenger transport, quiet, comfortable travel with luxury and spacious surroundings very much like a cruise ship. This prototype is set up for passenger and light freight for example;
2. Heavy cargo carriers operating point-to-point between manufacturer and end-user which eliminated intermediary load transfers

enroute as currently existed with rail cargo. In Cargo Mode, this cabin is replaced by a large cargo hold which can be attached and detached as required;

3. Capabilities of serving remote and/or unimproved sites not adequately served by other modes of transportation;

4. Disaster relief in inaccessible areas with room for extended medical facilities;

5. As stable platforms with long-term endurance for military intelligence, surveillance & reconnaissance such as with maritime surveillance, border patrol and search and rescue; and for

6. High altitude regional communications.

Sir Ewan also went on to explain that airships are greatly energy efficient as they do not rely on most of their power for lift. Moreover, using the latest solar power configurations, there is little or no carbon footprint. He also explained that in both the cargo and passenger configurations there is considerable flexibility in how deliveries or set downs could be achieved. In both cases, he emphasised, the *Orion* could deliver its precious cargos without landing as it carries a small fixed-wing electrically powered aircraft which can carry four passengers and their luggage. In addition, he continued, there were six, heavy-duty drones which could be used to accurately deliver cargo.

He waited until the advantages outlined on the screen made the appropriate impact on his audience. He then turned and looked at the small group of people who sat a short distance to his left.

"Now, let me introduce my very important team who have been instrumental in the planning and construction of this great airship." He looked around and beckoned to a large man standing with the small group of people who had assembled at the front of the cabin.

"First up, I would like to introduce you to Mr Edward Campbell who has been my Chief Engineer for some time. Ted?"

"Thank you, Sir Ewan." The engineer took his place at the lectern whilst Sir Ewan took a seat. "Well, now. Where to begin? I heard someone say 'Zeppelin' when I was walking down the centre aisle and so the first thing that I must do then is to make some comparisons. So now." he took up some papers which had been placed on the lectern and adjusted his spectacles.

"Now it's been a considerable time since the Count von Zeppelin launched his own famous airship – over one hundred years ago; to be exact in 1928. This was the dirigible the *Graf Zeppelin*. There had been others before that, but I won't go into their use during the Great War nor the other dirigibles used by other counties. No. The *Graf Zeppelin* was perhaps the first airship to show how one could travel around the world in safety and luxury. Despite the beginning of the Great Depression and growing competition from fixed-wing aircraft, the *Graf Zeppelin* regularly flew across the Atlantic from Germany to Brazil transporting an increasing volume of passengers and mail every year until 1936. Unfortunately, the following year, its bigger successor, the *Hindenburg* crashed in flames upon landing at Lakehurst in New Jersey and put the end to luxury airship travel." He looked up at the audience and realised that his last remark had caused some discomfort.

"Och, now! Never fear! No such thing will happen to the *Orion*. You see, the *Hindenburg* and most other Zeppelins used highly inflammable hydrogen gas for lift. We use the non-inflammable helium gas instead. But let me explain some of the other differences between your concept of the earlier Zeppelins and our modern airship, although the main similarity is that both the *Graf Zeppelin* – let's not talk about the *Hindenburg* – and the *Orion* are both dirigibles. That is, they have a rigid frame construction which contain the gas cells which give them their lift. They are not the non-rigid blimps which are simply gas bags attached to some small cabin or fuselage. So, what are some of the improvements of the *Orion*: Firstly, as I have said, we use helium gas for lift. This is not as buoyant as hydrogen but it does not burn. Indeed, it will not support burning at all. I'll not bore you with all of the technical details about helium, simply to say that is, unfortunately not as easily found as hydrogen and so it is more expensive. For many years, the United States produced more than 90% of commercially usable helium in the world from their oil and gas fields, while some plants in Canada, Poland, Russia, Algeria, Qatar and here in Australia have produced the remainder. So then, whilst using helium is much safer, Sir Ewan has had considerable problems obtaining it and paying for it."

There was some quite laugher from the audience and a wry smile from Sir Ewan sitting nearby.

"But I digress. I will let our tame boffin; Dr. Sinclair sort out the future problems with the scarcity of helium and our energy needs." He looked across to the young man sitting nervously with the rest of the team and then continued.

Secondly, you have probably noticed that the *Orion* is not the traditional cigar shape of the old Zeppelins. Good for their day as that shape had a certain amount of wind resistance. The *Orion* is constructed as a lifting body; that is, its shape will also help it rise as it pushes through the air – the same principle as an aircraft's wing. This also reduces some independence from the sole use of helium for lift. You might call its shape a delta wing but rather thick if you like – our workers colloquially refer to her as Fat Delta." There was some laughter from the audience and a depreciating smile from Sir Ewan. The engineer continued:

"Thirdly, the Zeppelins relied upon diesel engines using oil combustion for their propulsion. For example, the *Hindenburg* was powered by four reversible 890 kW   Daimler-Benz engines in fixed pods attached to the lower sides of the craft which gave the airship a maximum speed of about 135 km/h.

The *Orion* also has its outer pods but there are six of these and they are the latest K-23 model Siemens ducted fan electric motors. Each is 1200 kW and totally emission free. Our power is obtained from our solar panels which you may have seen on the upper part of the airship with supplementary power at night coming from a bank of low weight lithium batteries in the hull. Moreover, each engine pod, being much smaller than those in the Hindenburg, can be swivelled around in any direction and so can also be used to help with lift and sideways propulsion as required. We have estimated during our wind-tunnel experiments that the *Orion* should be able to achieve a maximum speed of about 200 km/hr. but general cruising would probably be about 150 km/hr.

Now my next point is rather interesting. It is where we have gone completely away from the traditional Zeppelin model. That is in the *Orion*'s construction."

A three-dimensional computer-generated image of the *Orion* came up on the screen. The engineer used his small handset to rotate the image around through several dimensions. He continued.

"You will remember that I said that the *Orion* was in fact shaped as a delta wing lifting body. Whereas the cigar-shaped Hindenburg had a length of 245 metres and a diameter of 41 metres, the *Orion* is 250 metres long from nose to the centre of its rear surface and 300 metres wide at its tail end. Hardly a long cigar, it is wider than it is long as one would expect from a delta-wing. The original *Hindenburg* was also of a duralumin construction, incorporating fifteen Ferris wheel-like main ring bulkheads along its length, braced to each other by longitudinal girders placed around their circumferences. Duralumin or 'durable-aluminium' as its name suggests is an alloy of lightweight aluminium with copper and traces of magnesium and manganese. The addition of the copper improves the aluminium's strength, but it does make the alloy susceptible to corrosion. Our major shift from such material – and I might add probably a huge shift away from our conventional thought in aircraft construction – is that the *Orion*'s framework is entirely of a geodesic monocoque design using bamboo rather than metal."

There were gasps from the audience and the young reporter from the *Herald* loudly called out:

"You mean that this airship is built of wood?"

The engineer waited until the hubbub had quietened out and then quietly spoke:

"No sir, it is made of grass, for that is what bamboo is, not a 'wood' in your terms. But if you all can hold your enthusiasm until later, I will let our esteemed guest, Mr. Zhan Yisheng explain all of that to you. What I would like to stress here is that our geodesic monocoque design means that the outer hull of the *Orion* is the airship's main supporting structure."

Using the handset, the engineer zoomed into the image on the screen which changed to reveal the internal construction of the hull. It consisted of a large number of inter-connected triangles which stretched completely over the outer surface of the airship. It was developed in the 20th century by American engineer and architect R. Buckminster Fuller. Of course, there have to be some internal bulkheads also made of thick girders of these triangles which also make up the containing frames for our twenty internal gas bags. Speaking of which,

I should also add that nine of these bags are partially filled and housed in our wings as it were. The other two are fore and aft inside the central construction and are what are termed 'balloonets' These are loosely-supported gas bags held within their relatively open frames. They can be filled with helium from our compressed gas tanks to gain extra lift or they can be emptied by compressing the gas back again to decrease lift. Being positioned in the stern and just and in the front of the central body, they can be used to maintain the overall horizontal position of the airship. Of course, we also carry the usual water buoyancy tanks which can be quickly emptied if we need to suddenly gain altitude."

The engineer took off his glasses and looked around at the audience who were now fully enthralled at the unique construction of the airship in which they sat.

"But enough from an old Scottish engineer who knows nothing about bamboo. Let me now introduce Mr. Zhan Yisheng of the Jīn Tàiyáng Engineering Company of Jiangsu to explain our use of this incredible material.

Mr Zhan who had been standing patiently to one side now stepped up to the lectern after giving a small bow to the engineer. He was taller than most Chinese and had a rather square, craggy face. "Almost Germanic-looking" thought the shallow young man from the *Herald*. Mr Zhan gave a bow to the audience and straightened a few papers which he had taken from a smart leather briefcase which he had lifted up to the lectern.

"Ha, ha!" he said in a nervous, slightly high-pitched voice." Please forgive, but I am not good in front of many people. Ha, ha. Thank you, Mr Campbell. Let me now show you how we made airship out of grass. Ha, ha."

There were smiles from the audience at this attempt at humour. Mr. Zhan continued.

"I am from the Jīn Tàiyáng Engineering Company of Jiangsu in China. I am not an engineer but a horticulturalist who grows things. At the Jīn Tàiyáng Engineering Company, we have specialised in growing and producing new types of bamboo for many different purposes. We have been doing that for over two hundred years. A long time, No? But we Chinese have been using bamboo in our constructions for thousands of years. Let me explain."

Taking the handset from the lectern, Zhan pointed it the screen which was filled with a large image of bamboo plants. He flicked through a number of images showing bamboo houses, furniture and finally scaffolding around modern high-rise buildings. He continued:

"Bamboo is evergreen perennial flowering plants of the subfamily Bambusoideae. They are of the grass family *Poaceae* and are the largest members of the grass family. Bamboo, is a natural fibrous material with a very high strength-to-weight ratio and so useful for structures. They also grow very, very, fast; some can grow up to 91 cm within a 24-hour period. Also, they have cylindrical-shaped stems which is a very, very strong shape. Yes, Mr Campbell?"

Zhan had turned and directed this comment to the engineer nearby.

"Oh, aye! Mr Zhan. That is correct. Tubes are much stronger than bars and girders."

"That is true. Thank you." Mr Zhan continued. "And we have shown that in, what you call tensile strength or the pulling apart, bamboo is stronger than steel. This is why we have been using it to build our high pagodas for centuries. Ha, ha!

The Germans used Duralumin in their Hindenburg. This alloy, which is light in weight, has a weight of 2780 kilograms for every cubic metre in volume. Our dry bamboo is only about 500 kilograms for every cubic metre. Much lower, yes? So! You see! We can make a big construction which is much lighter than that which Germans make in their airships. Ha, ha."

"But Duralumin can be welded very strongly. How do you hold your bamboo together?" asked the young reporter from the *Herald*.

Mr Zhen gave a polite bow towards the reporter and gave a wry smile.

"Ah! Thank you very much for asking that question. This is one of the main achievements of the Jīn Tàiyáng Engineering Company. Let me explain.

We grow bamboo very quickly. We can harvest it at any diameter from little pieces no bigger than your finger to several tens of centimetres across. And to any length up to about thirty metres. In our usual construction as geodesic type, we usually use lengths about one metre and diameter of about ten centimetres but we can use any size we like. So! How do we stick it together you ask? Well, that is our special treatment."

Mr Zhan clicked the slides back to the shape of a geodesic structure and looked back to the audience.

"Look carefully where the straight bits join. They are in triangles all joined at points. Yes? We call these joins 'hubs'. They can be flexible or rigid but in this airship, they are mostly rigid. The triangles come out of these hubs at different angles depending upon how many triangles there are and the curve needed for the overall surface. In metal construction, they could be split cylinder rings or several angled bars which are inserted into the metal pipe. What we do is grow our hubs to the required size, shape and number of joins needed. Yes. Grow!

Usually at the end of each set of a triangle section there will be the need for a hub joining five sections at a low angle but identical angle for each. We grow these hubs from bamboo. When the young plant shoots and gets to a small size, we insert small platinum frames made up of small, sharp plates set at the right angle for a five-join hub. The bamboo shoot quickly grows around the frame and forms five new stems. These we allow to grow until their diameter is just a little bigger than that of the rods of the triangle side so that they can fit inside the openings of the hub once we have removed the sap and other material inside the bamboo rods. We can then fasten the connection together with metal rivets or glue it with very strong cellulose fibre glues which make the joins as strong as the bamboo tube itself. It becomes one big piece. Ha, ha. Thank you".

Zhan gave a formal bow and smile to the audience and stepped back from the lectern. Sir Ewan quickly walked up and put his arm around his guest.

"Wait a minute, Yisheng. You forgot the rest of the contribution which your company has made to Project Orion. May I?" he said putting his open hand out to the lectern. Zhan bowed again and stepped aside as Sir Ewan once more stepped up to the lectern.

"I'm an old aeronautical engineer as you may know, so I can explain the work that Mr. Zhan's people have been doing on the other parts of the *Orion*. Indeed, without their help, the *Orion* would only be a series of connected engines, wires and secondary fittings. Let me explain.

What you have seen so far, the hull and a little of its interior is also the result of the experimental work and manufacturing expertise of the Jīn Tàiyáng Engineering Company. Let's take the hull for instance. As Mr Zhan explained, it is has a framework of strong and elaborately fixed bamboo as a geodesic structure. This is also covered by very thin panels of bamboo cloth, finely meshed together so that it is both lighter and stronger than the cotton used in earlier airships like the *Hindenburg*."

"But isn't bamboo inflammable?" interjected the young reporter from the *Herald*.

Sir Ewan looked over at the young man and smiled. "Certainly, it is highly inflammable in its usual state, but all of our bamboo frame components, the fabric of the hull, our cabin walls and indeed the bamboo laminated seat on which you now sit have all been treated with fire retardant before they have been assembled. We use a very successful product especially made for us by Dupont which is essentially a Boracic Acid/Borax preparation – the element Borax being found to be highly resistant to flame as it combines with its host material to form a barrier against fire."

"Isn't there a theory that the Hindenburg burnt because of its hull and not its hydrogen gas?" interjected a young woman who sat next to the *Herald* reporter.

"Yes, you are correct in that assumption, young lady. Some recent studies showed that the cotton fabric skin of the Hindenburg was doped with a material to waterproof, heat proof it and to give additional strength. The material they used included an aluminumized solution of cellulose nitrate – you may know of it as 'guncotton' used in explosive shells – moreover, the interior of its hull was painted with iron oxide. Put this together with powdered aluminium and you have a thermite mixture which burns giving molten iron and is used in joining railway tracks. A most explosive combination!

Have no fear. The *Orion* is made of different material. As I mentioned before, the basic fabric of the hull is physically-pressed bamboo. This is made from the youngest of plants so that the fibres are fine. They are then physically sorted and pressed together, not woven like most bamboo material which becomes like its cellulose cousins simply a rayon fibre. Am I right, Mr Zhan?"

Mr Zhan gave Sir Ewan and smile and bowed.

"To go on, the thin strips of bamboo cloth are treated against fire as I have explained and are then, given a very thin coating of aluminium using a vapourizing technique. This gives high reflexibility against heat and ultraviolet damage as well as being a strong covering over our framework when stretched.

I might also add, getting back to fire-proofing, that in the *Hindenburg*, any flame due to hydrogen gas combustion would have come from that expelled when landing. The gas itself will not burn except when combined with oxygen. In the *Orion* we use helium gas which has less lifting power but is inflammable mixed with any gases. Now, are there any other questions?"

The young reporter and his friend remained silent and no one else had any questions.

"Good!" said Sir Ewan. "I will now hand over to our scientific advisor, Dr. Paul Sinclair who will briefly, I hope, tell you about our use of power in the *Orion*. Paul?"

A slim young man with a shock of jet-black hair came slowly over to the lectern.

"Make it quick, Paul!" said Sir Ewan in a low voice. The young man gave a slight nod of his head in reply. He always felt uncomfortable around his employer; their personalities could not be anymore different. Whilst Sir Ewan Hunter had a strong, extroverted personality, Dr. Paul Sinclair tended to be quiet and uncomfortable around others. His studies had been the lifeboat which had taken him away from the pressures and boisterous nature of modern society.

"Umm..um" he stammered as he looked down at his brief notes on the lectern. After a brief pause, he looked up and in a quiet voice which needed all the power of the lectern microphone he began:

"Umm..um. Well. Umm. Firstly, I had better tell you about the helium shortage which Sir Ewan spoke about, but that is not what I wanted to speak about. Umm..helium comes from some oil wells, mainly in the United States and some of the other countries which Sir Ewan mentioned. It is also found in air as a rare gas at only 5.2 parts per million but being lighter than air, it can easily leak out into space and be lost forever. The helium that we find on earth is a product of radioactive decay from minerals made of uranium and thorium deep within the earth. These emit alpha particles composed of two protons and two neutrons, which then attract electrons turning into them into helium atoms. Some of it migrates upwards and may stay for a while in some natural oil and gas traps. These are where we get our helium gas from now, though the helium-producing wells are uncommon and most are being exhausted at a great rate. In the past, technological limits meant that helium was only economically recoverable at low concentrations - about 0.3% with the vast majority of the helium in gas reserves simply vented away. Today, we have found further supplies of natural gas containing commercially-recoverable amounts of helium in new wells in north-western Western Australia in the Buonaparte Gulf and northern Carnarvon Basins. We can also import helium from the vast oil and gas fields of Tanzania's Rift Valley, so we do not see a major problem in the future. We have done a few test trials here and have found that we that very little of this precious gas leaks from our permanent gas bags." He looked down at his notes and sorted out another sheet of paper and then looked back at his audience hoping that there would be no interjections or questions. He continued:

"umm..um. Let me now..ah tell you about our power usage in the *Orion*. We have six electric engines from Siemens each with a maximum power rating of 1200 kW. But we rarely would use them at full power. We think that we would obtain our best cruising speed of about 150 km/hr at probably three-quarters of our total power. That is, about 5400 kW total requirements. You may have seen when you came in that the upper surface of the *Orion*'s hull is a rather nice shiny dark blue colour. This is due to the ninety solar voltaic panels on its upper surface. These are our main source of power – coming directly from the Sun."

Some of the audience looked at each other and nodded approval at this use of free solar energy, a major development over the last fifty years as part of the renewable replacement for the old fossil fuels. The young scientist continued,

"But …um..these panels are nothing like the ones which have been on your houses for many years. They are the most advanced generation of flexible photovoltaic panels using polycrystalline silicon wafers which are typically only about 200 micrometres thick – not much thicker than a human hair. They are also much bigger than your average rigid silicon panel and we have been able to partially weave them into the thin, doped bamboo fabric of the rest of the hull. Whilst each small segment of each panel produces electricity at full sunlight of only a few volts, we have wired the panels on the upper surface of the *Orion* so that they will eventually produce a current at about 45 volts. Whilst the current is rather high, the relatively low voltage also reduces the chance of electrical arcing and so limits the risk of fire. In addition, we have installed a bank of the latest lithium-sulfur solid state batteries which do not use the risky lithium hexafluorophosphate electrolyte, which posed a fire and toxicity hazard in the older batteries. We also have a small bank of older liquid-filled lithium batteries using highly conductive fluorinated solvents with lithium ions which have low risk when it comes to a fire. These we use only as a backup as our primary bank of solid-state batteries are able to store excess solar voltaic charge during the day and are used to run our engines during the night – albeit at a much-reduced capacity. This is another reason for our initial routes being from the here to Western Australia as we have the biggest mining potential of lithium salts in the world being exploited in that state." He put down the paper he was reading from and looked up at the audience: "You will find all of the technical details in the Information Guide in your package. Thank you."

Sir Ewan gave the young scientist a weak smile and stepped back up to the lectern:

"Finally, and certainly not the least in our introduction as you will soon understand, is our Captain and his flight crew."

A small group of men and women who had been standing discretely well over to one side now came forward. They were dressed in the light blue uniforms of Hunter Aviation which were the same as most flight crews seen on the company's aircraft. One tall, blonde headed man wearing the golden 'scrambled egg' pattern on the peak of his cap and four golden rings on the sleeves of his jacket joined Sir Ewan at the lectern. Sir Ewan greeted the aviator with a broad grin and firm handshake before turning once more to the microphone:

"Let me introduce you to the man who will be taking us aloft tomorrow, our chief pilot and commander of the *Orion*, Captain Felix Eichner."

There was an enthusiastic applause from the audience as Captain Eichner stepped up to the microphone.

"I might add" - Sir Ewan continued "- that we were lucky enough to lure Captain Eichner away from Zeppelin Luftschifftechnik, the successor of the original company which built those early airships so famous, or perhaps infamous, in history. That company, as you may know has been operating small semi-rigid on domestic route within Germany and some neighbouring countries – more like local bus lines than international air transportation. The good captain, here was very glad to join us and carry the concept of the airship to its former intent. Captain Eichner."

More applause as Captain Eichner took the microphone. He was a tall man with a sharp, intelligent face with blue eyes which seemed to be a perfect match for his immaculate uniform.

"Thank you, Sir Ewan." He said in perfect English with only a slight hint of his north German accent. "yes, you are right! It has been a long time since airships once again took to the international skies and I am pleased now to be a part of it. But I digress. I fly airships not make the speeches; you understand. Let me introduce my crew." Captain Eichner turned and raised his arm up to indicate his flight crew who had now formed a line facing the audience.

"Firstly, there is my First Officer and second-in-command Helmuth Zabel, also a emigrant from Zeppelin Luftschifftechnik who can fly airships almost as good as me."

The officer name gave a quick smile and a short bow to the audience. The captain continued:

Next there is Second Officer Heather Conrad who is from your own country and has been especially trained in Germany to fly airships. But here she will drive us on the right side of the road. Ja?"

 There was some laughter at this little joke and a wry smile from Heather.

"Now a most important man who will keep all of our engines running, our Flight Engineer Nigel Stenlake who comes to us from the De Haviland Company in Britain. Of course, all of our German manuals have been translated into English and there are plenty of pictures."

Flight Engineer Stenlake almost seemed to be a replica of Project Orion's Chief Engineer Ted Campbell; about fifty years old, stocky and with a confident expression on his tanned broad face. He rolled his eyes at his commander's little jest and it was now clear to the audience that the Flight Crew had a good rapport with their commander.

"Now this will be short flight but if we get lost, we have our local fellow, Navigator Mike Newcombe. He assures me that if the GPS units break down, he carries a road directory of this state in his pocket.

The important people I have left until last. Here is our Chief Purser John Andrews who we have shanghaied – is that the expression? John previously worked as the Senior Purser (Administration) in the main office of a well-known shipping company after many years at sea onboard cruise ships. His work here will be very similar and he assures me that he does not get airsick. So far so good. He has several junior staff to help him with all of the good things you will like to eat, drink – and I hope buy when we take off. To help him around the *Orion* we have many happy staff who will look after you and they are under the watchful care of our two Chief Stewards, Dorothy McGuire and Donald Kemp."

The last three Flight Crew linked arms and gave a big wave to the audience. Captain Eichner once more turned to Sir Ewan and shook his hand before returning to his little group.

"Thank you, Captain Eichner and your crew. You see, Ladies and Gentlemen that we are in very good and experienced hands. There are many more people, of course who help look after our airship and its passengers. We have riggers, electricians, cargo masters and others who work behind the scenes and who you will probably not run into but now, let us look towards our flight tomorrow." Sir Ewan again raised his arm to acknowledge the members of Project Orion who had been introduced and they left via the central aisle of the cabin to the applause of the audience.

"In a moment our group leaders will take you for a quick tour of the main passenger areas so please remember your colours and stay with the group. Security is very tight here, so we don't want any one wandering about. After the tour, they will take you back to the main building for a very sumptuous supper and then we will show you to your sleeping quarters so that you will be wide awake when we have our launch at eight tomorrow. Good night ladies and gentlemen."

4.

Julie Wright, the PR Director had walked over in front of the audience as most of the project team retired to the back of the cabin.

"Now, ladies and gentlemen, we are going to take you on a very short tour of the main parts of the *Orion*. Naturally, for security reasons we cannot take you below to the control cupola nor up into the main superstructure of the airship, but we will give you a good idea of public and passenger areas which you will enjoy tomorrow at launch. You have been assigned a tour group leader in either blue or green colours. They are waiting at the rear of the cabin, so if you would kindly make your way to where they are situated, we will get on with the tour at the end of which they will take you back to the main building."

The members of the audience slowly stood up and found their way to the rear of the cabin where they found the tour group leaders. The two hostesses, for they both served in that capacity in Hunter Aviation's H-jets, stood on either side at the rear bulkhead. They held small flags; one light blue and the other a light green, the colours of their parent company.

"This way, Greens!" called one.

"Over here, Blues!" called the other.

The green leader turned and walked up a wide, central flight of stairs which led to the next deck above and her small group followed. The blue leader walked along the rear bulkhead until she came to a wide arch which contained a roller door which she opened electrically using a push button. It opened to reveal a brightly lit corridor into which she walked.

The young reported from the *Herald* was in the blue group and quickly moved up to the front of the small crowd so that he could hear everything which his group leader would say and to be able to ask her questions if needed.

They walked through the wide roller door which opened out into a large area which reminded the reporter of a warehouse. The leader stopped and turned towards her audience.

"This is our Secondary Storage Facility or SSF. When we are in Passenger Mode as we are tonight, this area will hold their luggage and some small amount of freight.

"Small amount! Ha!" thought the young man from the Herald because the SSF was as big as most warehouses he had seen even if it was only two stories in height.

The group leader moved on through the empty storage area and opened another large roller door in the rear bulkhead.

"We are now going to enter what I think is the most exciting part of the *Orion*; the hangar."

There were gasps of astonishment as the group moved into another large space which even larger than the storage space from which they came. It was probably as big as a tennis court and two storeys in height. In the centre of the floor was a large circular space separated into two semi-circles, each marked yellow and set slightly below the rest of the floor space. They appeared to be doors which could be retracted into spaces below the rest of the floor. Signs with red around their edges warned that there was no admittance unless authorised. However, the most striking thing about this room, which was indeed a hangar, was the small light aircraft with folded wings which hung securely from a crane-like structure above.

"This is our little taxi service!" she laughed. "If you will excuse the pun, we can drop off up to four passengers and their luggage anywhere en route without having to take the *Orion* down to land."

Under her direction, the group moved around on the outer side of the yellow circle.

"As you can see," she continued, "our little taxi would be lowered to the floor so that its passengers and luggage can be loaded for the flight. It could also be used for a small amount of freight and mail deliveries. When all is ready, the pilot can open the hangar doors and the rack crane will lower it below the airship which naturally will slow right down to almost a stop. He would then unfold the wings electronically and the aircrew above will check that they have locked into position. Only then will he start the aircraft's electric motor and release what we called the sky hook, which releases the aircraft. When the aircraft returns, the reverse procedure is put into operation, so that we can also take onboard new passengers, mail or a small amount of freight from below; especially from remote communities such as cattle stations and mining camps."

"Tell us about the aircraft," spoke up the young man from the *Herald* who had taken up the role of the group's spokesperson.

The young hostess smiled and quickly took out a small brochure from her pocket.

"I'm glad you asked that question," she said. "As you can see, it is a modified version of the Cessna Electrofan light aircraft. It is powered by a 650 kW Siemens ducted fan electric motor and has an eight-hundred-kilogram payload capacity. It has a maximum speed of one hundred knots – about 150 km/hr and a range of about 500 kilometres on its four light-weight solid state lithium-sulfur batteries. She can easily catch up to the *Orion* after a drop off, so it can be then collected, stored and recharged for its next mission. With our advanced RADAR and GPS facilities, the *Orion Mini* or just *Mini* as she is known can be used at any time that there is a need to connect to the ground."

"This is not a new concept!" spoke up the young reporter in a cynical tone.

The hostess smiled again, looking directly at the young man.

"Indeed, you are perfectly correct sir. The United States government built the USS *Akron* and the USS *Macron* over one hundred years ago as helium-filled rigid airship on the Zeppelin model as flying aircraft carriers. They carried up to five F9C Sparrowhawk fighter biplanes which could be launched and retrieved from the mothership."

"Yeah! But didn't they both crash?" said the young reporter.

"Unfortunately, you are right again, sir. The Akron crashed in 1933 and the Macron two years later. Both due to severe storms."

"So, what happens if history repeats itself with the *Orion*?" the young reported said with a smirk on his face.

The hostess again smiled. "That would be highly unlikely sir. The *Orion* is stronger and has more powerful engines than those old Zeppelin designs. Moreover, we will be travelling routes across a continent not noted for its severe storms and our advanced links to all of the meteorological RADAR sites across the country means that we avoid storm cells and even winds which are unfavourable. Like the old sailing ships, we would tend to go around any adverse weather. This is what the old *Graf Zeppelin* did on its many successful flights across the stormy Atlantic. Should this be impossible, we could even rise above most storms as the central sections of the *Orion* are pressurised like conventional aircraft. Are there any more questions?"

The young reporter kept silent. He knew that his group leader had been chosen for her ability to handle people and had all of the answers at hand.

The hostess also opened another large roller door set into the rear of the hangar. It contained four large devices consisting of metal frameworks having four ducted propellors and a central box-like centre. These rested on their wheels or hung on a large rack crane in the roof of this mini hanger. She explained that these were the latest in cargo drones; each one being the capacity of carrying about 500 kg in cargo which could be loaded and dropped through the central hatchway and remotely piloted to recipients on the ground below. They could also be sent to retrieve cargo as required. There was a small glass cubicle in the corner of the hangar which contained the drone pilot's controls.

"Well, then ladies and gentlemen. We have seen all that we can on this deck – there is only the control cupola for our aircrew who will operate the airship which is directly forward of the flight cabin in which we were seated before. We can now go up one of the crew gangways to the main deck or deck 2 above us to see how the *Orion*'s passengers will be accommodated.

Meanwhile, the Blue Group had been taken up the broad, carpeted stairwell which led up from the centre of the rear bulkhead of the large Flight Cabin. At the top of the stairs, the members of the group were all amazed at the large, well-lit space into which they walked. It was not unlike the atrium of some large cruise liner in so much as it rose up to several decks around an elongated oval space. The front and part of the forward ceiling of this atrium was clear plexiglass which now looked out onto the darkened airfield beyond. It was, however illuminated by many small lights and spotlights which clearly showed its cavernous interior. The floor of this space also resembled a large atrium of any prestigious cruise liner. There were comfortable lounge chairs, tables and even a few potted palms. Further up front and below the huge glass windows of the nose of the airship, there were two observation areas in which passengers could sit and watch the expected views below. Around the sides of the central lounge area were several smaller rooms including what was obviously two bars, a coffee lounge, gift shop and across from them what was obviously a long purser's desk. All of these were yet to be completely fitted out and were now empty of their crew and stock, but the opulence was still very obvious.

The Blue Leader assembled the group into the centre of the main lounge and pointed to the large circular stair well which rose up to the higher decks.

"Welcome to the main deck which is actually the second level of the *Orion*. Here we will have all of the creature comforts of our airship. Here you can meet your friends, have a leisurely coffee and cake or even purchase some souvenirs of your flight. Above us you can see our two accommodation decks, decks three and four. We will be going up there soon but if you follow me, we will go aft and visit the dining room.

Several of the guests commented on the similarities between this vast area and those of cruise lines in which they had sailed. Indeed, going through the two glass double doors into the dining room also reminded them of dining in style at sea. This room was also spacious but was only of a single story. The many circular tables, some in bays around the side, but most in the centre of the room did resemble a liner's first-class dining room. The walls were all wood-panelled and hung with prints of earlier balloons and airships. The carpet was blue as before and there were glass and shining chrome serving stations at various places around the area.

"I'm sorry that we cannot take you for a guided tour of the kitchens, but they are rather cramped for movement but through those revolving doors at the rear of the dining room. In there we have all of the modern conveniences and of course, it is an all-electric kitchen. Now, let's retrace our steps and go up to one of the upper accommodation decks."

Holding up her little blue flag, she walked back through the group and out into the large atrium. They followed her up the ornate, wide, curved stairway to the deck above. On this deck, with its polished bamboo railing going all the way around the atrium, was a wide, light-green carpeted walkway which contained several small bays of lounge chairs and tables. There were also some smaller tables positioned at the railing so that guests could view the activities below on the atrium floor. There was also a small, bar at the stern end of the opening. In front, the huge plexiglass windows of the airship's nose now showed a clear night sky outside. As almost by design, the bright constellation of Orion sparkled in the dark sky.

Walking along the deck, the hostess opened one of the many small doors which were along the sides of the walkway.

"Here is a typical cabin," she said, standing aside so that her group could look into the small room. "Not quite as big as a ship's cabin because space is still at a premium on board an airship, but you can see that it is well-appointed never-the-less."

Members of the group took their turn looking into the cabin. It seemed to be about ten metres long and about five metres wide. On one side was a double bunk made of highly-polished bamboo with a small ladder at the far end. On the other side was a long vanity unit which also included a wash basin and a long mirror stretching along its length. There was a crystal water jug with two classes held firmly in a silver holder on its top and a small bar refrigerator below it. A wide, open-faced cupboard with a blue and green patterned curtain filled the space from the vanity unit to the cabin door. Between the bunks and the vanity unit was a large porthole with side curtains also in the same blue and green fabric and below it was a small desk and wicker chair. A small white telephone and a black information folder sat upon the desk."

"No en-suite on this deck, I'm afraid. There are several first-class cabins way forward which do have a very small en suite unit and a queen-sized bed, but the passengers in the tourist class cabins on this deck and the one above must use the four washrooms which are at the rear of each of the two decks. There are also two washrooms off the main deck below."

"How many passengers can the *Orion* carry?" asked a rather stout lady who now occupied most of the cabin door.

"At a full load, we can carry 28 first-class passengers and up to 92 tourist-class passengers; the latter being in two and some four-berth cabins. That is 120 passengers, which would be considered our maximum capacity with a crew of 40."

"That's a large crew for an aircraft!" spoke up an older man standing outside the cabin door.

"It is, sir – for an aircraft, but the *Orion* should be considered more like a ship – an airship in fact – than one of our H-jet airliners. The *Orion* will also operate like a ship and you will find that the crew has many duties like that on board a cruise liner. We have our purser staff such as those at the front desk and two chefs with their staff in the dining room and cafes as well as our flight crew of six and a number of engineers and riggers who maintain the engines and the airship's hull. Are there any questions?"

There were a few simple questions from the group, mainly about the furnishings which were mostly bamboo and bamboo fabric as well as the amount of water carried and the type of food served aboard; the later from the stout lady who had occupied most of the cabin doorway during the talk.

The group leader took her people back down the stairwell where they passed the Green Group going upstairs to view the cabins. She then followed the previous route of the other group down through the crew stairway and into the hanger where her people were amazed at the facilities there.

Sir Ewan Hunter walked up the carpeted stairway which led up to the observation deck in the clear glass nose of the airship. He had a confident smile on his weather-beaten face and was content that all was going to plan. He observed the tour groups as they wandered about the main deck of the airship, gazing in wonder at the lounges, bars and many small shops which would be soon available to passengers. On the observation deck, he looked down on the main atrium of the *Orion* at the people below. There had been stifled cries of awe as each group had come up the main entrance and onto the main deck; even the loud-mouth young reporter from the Herald had simply stood silently with his mouth open.

It was then that he noticed his chief engineer, Ted Campbell and another man whom he recognised as Bill Summerville, one of the foremen coming across from one of the access doors on the far side of the observation deck. Campbell did not look happy.

"We've got another dose of sabotage, Sir Ewan!" he said even before he had come up to the CEO. Without waiting for any acknowledgement, the engineer turned to the other man and said:

"Go on, Bill. Tell Sir Ewan what you found."

Summerville, who was indeed the main foreman of the team of expertly-trained riggers who were responsible for much of the framework and supporting struts and wires within the *Orion*'s hull looked concerned, both at what he had to say and being in the presence of the CEO of the company. After a short intake of breath, he began:

"Well, it's like this, Sir Ewan. I had finished my work on one of the stern steering mechanisms – the port tail fin to be precise, and had come down to check the work sheets of my riggers. I did that tail job myself because the mechanism there is rather intricate and needed some special attention, if you'd forgive my boasting. It was only just a short while ago when I went back to the engineering office and to get my test meter which I use to confirm the conductivity of the solenoids used in the *Orion*'s controls that I realised that I must have left it at my earlier work near the tail fin."

"Get on with it, man!" Sir Ewan snapped impatiently." The foreman looked across at the engineer and continued.

"Well Sir Ewan, when I finally climbed back up to the tail fin area, I saw that the solenoid which controls the port tail fin had been smashed. Unnatural like. All wires and broken pieces of metal like it had been hit several times with a hammer. Some of the main control wires had been cut too!"

Sir Ewan looked at his Chief Engineer and then back at the foreman:

"Thank you, Mr. Summerville. I am sorry that I was a little impatient with you. Please forgive me. This was not news which I wanted to hear at this late hour in our project launch proceedings." He turned quickly back to the engineer.

"Can it be fixed before our guests climb aboard at eight tomorrow, Ted?"

"Difficult to say, Sir Ewan. Bill and I would have to take a better look at the damage before we can answer that question, but we carry plenty of spares including solenoids…"

"Too right, Ted!" interjected the foreman with some renewed enthusiasm. "It didn't look like whoever did it was much of a technical hand as the main section which forms the base of the control mechanism was untouched. It contains all of the electronics needed to operate the system."

"Good!" replied the CEO with a grim smile. "Get on to it, please Ted and I'll get Troy Jaeger and his team to do a thorough search of the other controls and sensitive areas of the hull. It's going to be a long night but the dawn will come quickly enough and as they say, 'fools look to tomorrow; wise men use tonight'. I'll be in my office if you need me."

5.

Jaeger was not very happy as he looked into the, dark brown surface scum on his morning coffee which had gone cold during his long breakfast. He had not had much sleep the previous night thanks to Sir Ewan's insistence of yet another full security sweep of the *Orion*. The man was too full of energy and seemed to be everywhere during Jaeger's own personal inspections, even up on top of the *Orion*'s hull where Jaeger was forced to wear a full EVA or Extra Vehicular Activity suit even including the oxygen mask when the airship was still on the ground.

"Go there, Jaeger! Look at that, Jaeger! Have you checked this and that out, Jaeger!" The demands of Sir Ewan in the many hours before dawn echoed in his fatigued brain and in his imagination seemed to ripple off the surface his cold coffee. No! Sir Ewan was much too glib in his conversation and over enthusiastic in his concerns about the *Orion*'s safety.

At least Ted Campbell was happy. Too happy. With Sir Ewan's hustle and bustle around the giant airship, Campbell had found all of the spare parts he needed and his over-worked team had finally repaired the damaged control mechanisms just before dawn. "Too easy!" Jaeger thought. The resident Boffin, Sinclair had been conspicuous by his absence. Jaeger had seen him only once going into the main battery room during his third inspection of the inner hull at Sir Ewan's insistence. He could do a lot of damage there.

His thoughts were interrupted by the loudspeakers which were part of the old mess hall's past life.

"Boarding will take place in twenty minutes please," came the well-modulated voice of PR Julie, "would guests please secure their rooms and report to their group leaders at the coloured exit points where boarding passes will be handed out. Thank you."

"Here we go. Off into the wild blue yonder!" thought Jaeger as he got up and went to his own room in the staff quarters. His suit jacket would be needed to help conceal his pistol as well as provide some warmth when aloft. He noticed as he walked outside and headed for the staff quarters that the Orion had been towed out of its hanger by its huge tractor and was now held down by mooring ropes on the tarmac in front of the hanger. Captain Eichner and his entire flight crew were now walking around the underside of the airship as part of their pre-flight check. "Good luck!" Jaeger thought to himself.

Soon, small groups had gathered at each of the main doors to the mess hall where their group leaders, conspicuous in their light blue Hunter Aviation uniforms and small coloured flags, were waiting. As each guest passed through the electronic surveillance portal, they were handed their small blue boarding pass and told that each had their allocated seat number written upon it and that boarding would be done, as before, up the wide main gangway.

The whole affair reminded Jaeger of a typical boarding sequence for any aircraft at any airport. He winked at the green group leader as he skirted the metal surveillance portal; no need to frighten the guests with the exposure of his firearm, not to mention the throwing knife strapped to his left leg below the leg of his immaculate Armani suit.

Everyone was excited about the impending flight of the giant airship and so they quickly moved down the aisles and found their numbered seats, directed by the cabin crew who stood at the top of each aisle. When everyone was seated, Julie Wright, now dressed in the Hunter Aviation uniform of senior cabin crew, walked into the front centre of the cabin and took up a microphone.

"Thank you, ladies and gentlemen. Welcome to the first passenger flight of Hunter Aviation's airship Orion. You are seated in the flight cabin of the airship; where all passengers would normally come on their arrival. In a moment, our cabin crew will run through the usual safety drill with the lifejackets which are under your seats. I am sure that most of you have seen all of this before when flying in aircraft now I must change tack, to use a nautical term, and go into lifeboat mode."

There were some quite conversation amongst the audience but she continued:

"Should we have an emergency onboard which requires evacuation, there will be three loud blasts on the Orion's siren – yes, like any good ship, we do have a very loud siren attached to the hull in case of fog when at low altitudes. There will also be a verbal warning on the airship's PA system asking all onboard to report here to their designated seats so it is important that you know your seat number. Once all are seated and have buckled up, there will be another warning over the PA system that the flight cabin will be ejected from the main hull. In a moment we will sound the warning alarm so please remember that this one is simply a drill." With that, she stepped away from the lectern and spoke into a small communicator to the flight crew controlling the airship. Suddenly from well above the flight cabin there came three loud and long blasts from what sounded exactly like a ship's foghorn. The lights in the flight cabin suddenly changed to the dull red of the emergency lighting and this was followed by the ringing of alarm bells and an equally loud message from the loudspeakers given in a soft female voice:

"For exercise! For exercise! Would all passengers report to their assigned seats in the flight cabin. Would all passengers report to their assigned seats in the flight cabin…." Julie spoke once more into her communicator and the bells and the warning message were suddenly cut off.

There was now some discussion from the audience and a few worried looks on some of their faces. Julie Wright smiled and held up her hand.

"Oh! Please do not worry about this event. Should it happen, I assure you that it would much less traumatic than a lifeboat launch from any large cruise ship. The doors to this cabin will be automatically closed, the explosive bolts holding this module to the main hull will explode – rather quietly I might add – and we will drop silently and smoothly from the hull. This soft launch will be done by drag chutes which will ease our rate of fall until the main parachutes will open and slowly carry us down to earth."

"Yeah! But what if we are over the sea?" shouted the young man from the Herald.

"That would not be a problem, sir," smiled Julie who hoped that in such an event the reporter would be thrown overboard. "The flight cabin is fully waterproofed and designed to act like a small boat. We have flotation sections in our lower hull, access hatches in the roof and our own small motor and batteries at its stern. There is also the usual EPIRP beacon which activates as soon as we come down on the water and there are enough emergency supplies to last a full complement for at least a week. Are there any more questions?"

The young reporter now had the attention of the rest of the guests and so he asked:

"So, what about the crew? Where do they get off?"

"Thank you for that question as we do value the safety of all onboard the Orion. With the exception of the crew on duty, usually the pilot and another officer, the rest of the crew, including the hull riggers and ancillary staff will report here just as you do. You may have noticed that the back few rows have been roped off for these people. On this flight, Captain Eichner and his First Officer Helmuth Zabel will be in command. In case of an emergency, once the passengers have been seated and their numbers checked by our electronic seat sensors, then the duty pilot will activate the ejection of the flight cabin. If they are unable to do this, then there is a timing mechanism which will carry out the ejection five minutes after the last evacuation warning. Naturally, if there is an immediate threat of crashing, then this mechanism can be overridden by the switches in the control cabin or in our master electrical room. The duty crew and any other member of the crew who may be required to stay aboard to assist in the evacuation of passengers have our light aircraft or parachutes with which to leave the airship. All of our crew have been trained in the use of parachutes and the pilots and several others of the flight crew are able to fly the Mini Orion." By now the audience had settled down and seemed quite comfortable with the safety procedures of the airship. Julie continued:

"By the way, if you see something which should cause our evacuation, you will find the usual glass-fronted alarm boxes all around the airship. These will activate an alarm in the duty crew area and so will be investigated before the main alarm is sounded. However, there are so many inbuilt safety features on board that such emergencies are unlikely to happen, especially on our short day trip which I hope that you will now enjoy. Thank you for your attention and patience and so now I will ask you to watch our cabin crew as they go about the usual aircraft lifebelt drill. Good morning."

With that, she resumed her seat in the front row along with the rest of the executives and fastened her seat belt and looked across the row to Sir Ewan who gave her a short nod and a 'well-done' smile.

Soon there was a slight vibration and passengers near the side portholes had the distinct but silent feeling that the buildings outside were slowly sinking into the ground. In fact, this was just an illusion as the Orion rose quietly and slowly off the tarmac.

Outside on the tarmac, the rest of Project Orion staff, both administration and engineering and ground personnel had all gathered to say farewell to the Orion. Amongst them was Mr. Zhan Yisheng, the bamboo engineer who suffered badly from airsickness and so had decided to stay on the ground and watch the giant airship lift off. It rose slowly and majestically from the old airstrip and began to gain height.

On board, the guests and crew sat comfortably in their chairs watching the early morning sunlit scenery on the large monitors which covered most of the cabin's front bulkhead. Very soon the 'fasten seat belts' signs on the front bulkhead went off and Sir Ewan's voice came over the PA system.

"Well, take-off successful! Please feel free now to undo your seat belts and move out of the cabin at your own leisure. You are free now to depart and move up the stairs to the main deck where you will find that the catering section of Hunter Aviation has put on a nice morning tea in the atrium. Thank you."

The guest slowly made their way out of the flight cabin and up into the huge, open space on the deck above. During the night, the catering staff and others from Hunter Aviation had fitted this area with potted palms and a large smorgasbord of pastries, sandwiches, cakes and other delicacies. A pianist had taken her place at a grand piano situated on a small dais in the centre of the atrium and now began playing. To many guests this was a totally wondrous feeling. To the front, beyond the raised viewing platform, they could see the small fluffy white cumulus clouds beginning to appear in the path of the airship whilst sipping perfectly brewed coffee and making a selection from of the many delicacies on offer. They now had the total freedom to wander about the atrium of the main deck or go up on top the forward observation platform to gaze on the countryside below which now appeared to be slowly drifting away from them. They were also pleased that the airship was incredibly stable without a hint of any motion other than that shown by the passing vista of the land below.

Sir Ewan walked slowly through the small groups of people, smiling and asking their opinion of the pleasant flight of the Orion. Most of the replies were remarks about the relative silence and smoothness of the flight. There were many comparisons with the huge, stabilized ocean liners which many of the well-heeled passengers had often experienced. Sir Ewan took all of these complements with a slight bow of his head and a reply such as:

"We do not have to worry about sea-sickness at 2000 metres and besides, how could you travel at over 100 kilometres an hour onboard a ship?"

The Orion now headed west across the extensive plains that lay beyond the Great Divide that separated them from the Tasman Sea well to the east. The weather had proven ideal for the first passenger voyage of the Orion; a blue sky except for a few fluffy white cumulus clouds with some tall thunderheads well off course to the south. The winds were gently blowing from the southwest, giving the airship a slight tailwind. Being away from the mountain range, there were no sudden updrafts or erroneous wind currents to affect the stability of the airship.

By now, most passengers had relaxed making the atmosphere more like that onboard a luxury cruise ship. Unfortunately, on this inaugural public relations flight, the many small shops, specialist cafes, health spas and restaurants had not yet been commissioned, but the catering staff of Hunter Aviation were well experienced in setting up long tables at the end of the atrium with the best in linen, glass and silverware. A variety of the best wines and foods had been brought onboard that morning in large hot and cold boxes. These were now being prepared by Hunter Aviation's head chef and his staff. Lunch was going to be a special occasion.

At precisely twelve thirty the announcement came over the PA system that lunch would now be served at the rear of the atrium and that guests should make their way there and be seated. The table was well set with the best of silverware and glassware. Freshly-cut flowers filled ornamental vases at various intervals along the table. Guests picking up the menus found that they were in for a treat:

Onboard the Orion inaugural flight

Appetisers and Soup
Australian Prawn Cocktail
Homemade Piccalilli
Escargot Bourguignons
Cream of Tomato Soup

Entrées
Pan-seared Scallops with Celeriac Purée
Paves of Australian Salmon
Dill Potatoes with Tomatoes and Sauce Maltaise
Buttered Asparagus Spears and Sauce Diane

Side Dishes
Steamed Vegetables of the Day
Baked Potato, Creamed Potatoes, French Fries

Desserts
Chocolate Orange Fallen Cake
French Vanilla Cream Broulee
Strawberry Cheesecake
International Cheese Trolley

There was also a very palatable wine list featuring some of the best and most expensive wines in the country. The luncheon went on for some time, during which Sir Ewan and some of the high-level guests stood up and gave short speeches. Sir Ewan's speech was mostly about the potential of the Orion and her sister airships in the long-haul passenger and freight opportunities, especially between the new inland mining ventures and the east coast. Enthusiastic replies came from some of the guests who had interests in mining and tourism, especially those whose companies had suffered after the international embargo on fossil fuels. After dinner, fine Turkish coffee was served up on the observation deck so that visitors could watch the afternoon sun painting the vast western plains. Things were going very well for Sir Ewan and Project Orion.

6.

The coffee had been excellent and the guests now sat about on the comfortable lounge chairs of the observation deck or were sitting below in the potted palm atrium listening to the music being played on the grand piano. The guests seated in the observation deck were greatly impressed by the vista of the vast, inland plain which stretched out across the plexiglass bow. The afternoon sunlight sparkled on the sinuous waterway of the Darling River and the Menindee Lakes beyond as the airship slowly began her turn back towards the east and her home base where she was expected to land in another five hours.

Suddenly the guests' feelings of comfort and relaxation were broken by three loud blasts on the airship's siren and the equally loud alarm bells and warning message sounding over the loud speakers. The red emergency lighting gave the atrium a soft warm glow which contrasted with the bright light still streaming through the plexiglass bow windows. Outside, the blades of the ducted fan electric motors stopped leaving the airship drifting in the still air.

"Would all passengers report to their assigned seats in the flight cabin. Would all passengers report to their assigned seats in the flight cabin..." which continued to sound as the panicked guests grabbed their belongings and rushed down the stairs of the observation deck and across the atrium. The pianist at the piano hurriedly slammed the lid of the keyboard shut, grabbed his sheet music folio and ran towards the broad stairway which led to the flight cabin.

This was no exercise but the real thing! The cabin staff had been trained in just such an emergency but now they waited impatiently at their various stations to reassure the guests and to direct them in an orderly manner down the broad stairway into the flight cabin and to their assigned seats. A few of the guests, who had forgotten their seat numbers looked perplexed and stood at the bottom of the stairway until a member of the cabin crew could look up their name on the lists that they carried. There was no major concern with this issue as the guests on this inaugural flight occupied only a fraction of the seats available in the flight cabin. The riggers and other crew of the Orion also entered the cabin through various service hatchways as well as down the main stairway. Sir Ewan, not one to panic in an emergency, now strode down the central aisle and stood in the centre front part of the cabin, a microphone in his hand:

"No need to rush, my friends. The Orion seems to be quite stable and we have plenty of time before the flight crew release our cabin." By now the emergency announcements had stopped but the alarm bells still rang out loud and clear.

Most of the guests had by now found their seats and were looking around the cabin apprehensively and talking anxiously to their neighbours. More than a few of the guests were distraught and had tears on their frightened faces.

A small group of the executive staff were now either helping nearby guests to fasten their seatbelts or attending to their own seating. Ted Campbell, the chief engineer was about to head off across the cabin and down through the open hatchway which led to the control cabin when he was stopped by Jaeger who had come from that direction.

"I wouldn't go down there, Chief," he said with a stern look on his face. "Captain Eichner and the first officer are both dead and the controls have been smashed. There's no one else down there, so I suggest that we look after the living."

The shocked look on the old engineer's face and his uncontrolled oath in broad Scots attracted the attention of Sir Ewan who was standing only a few paces away.

"What's this, Jaeger?" he said as he came up to the two men.

"Dead, Sir Ewan. The captain and the first officer. Who's missing from our people here?" he said, looking past the belligerent face of Sir Ewan and around the immediate part of the flight cabin where the main staff were now seating themselves. Sir Ewan, now totally flustered, also looked around and stammered:

"Why....um. I'm not sure."

"Paul Sinclair is not here," interjected the engineer. "I saw him about an hour ago and he told me that he had to go aloft to the outer hull to check on some of the solar arrays which were not up to scratch."

Jaeger reached into his coat and made a show of checking his holstered SIG Sauer P365 pistol. "Well, now at least we know the identity of our saboteur. I never did trust Sinclair. He always seemed to know more than he should." There was a slight pause and Jaeger looked firmly at Sir Ewan. "Not to worry. I can handle him before he does some more damage to the Orion. With that he walked swiftly up the main aisle towards the stairway to the main deck and one of the service hatchways which led up past the passenger accommodation and into the main cavern-like interior of the airship's hull.

Sir Ewan looked aghast at the engineer with his mouth open as words now had failed him when suddenly an unexpected further emergency announcement came over the loud speaker:

"Fasten seat belts! Fasten seat belts! The safety capsule will be ejected in thirty seconds." This message continued to be broadcast as the emergency doors around the flight cabin suddenly began to slide shut, completely separating the cabin from the rest of the airship. Unnoticed in the new period of panic, second officer Heather Conrad, who had been seated with the rest of the off-duty flight crew next to the hatchway to the control cabin, suddenly unbuckled her seat belt and threw herself through the closing hatchway. Seeing Jaeger emerge from the control cabin and the shock on Sir Ewan's face meant that something was wrong. Sir Ewan looked startled and turned to his chief engineer:

"What tha'! This is not supposed to happen until the release switch is thrown or after the time delay!"

The old engineer had sat down and was quickly fastening his seat belt:

"Aye! That's right Sir Ewan. It's only when the airship is in imminent danger of crashing when the time delay is overridden. Someone has activated the override switch in the control room or up in the main switchboard room up yonder." He swept his had up to point to the rear of the cabin where the main switchboard was located in a secure room at the top of the main stairway in the passageway leading to the atrium.

"11, 10, 9, 8, 7, 6, 5, 4, 3, 2, 1, capsule ejecting. Capsule ejecting," came the soft unruffled female tones of the recorded warning message.

There were a series of muffled explosions around the sides of the cabin and suddenly the feeling that one gets in a high-speed elevator when it suddenly drops. The flight cabin, now the safety capsule, dropped away from the airship with its bright orange drogue chutes trailing behind and now starting to blossom open to slow the descent of the capsule. Almost immediately after they had been fully deployed and the capsule slowed to a constant rate of fall, the two large main parachutes began to untangle themselves from their containers to bring the safety capsule to a soft landing.

Paul Sinclair liked being outside the airship and up on her broad, V-shaped upper surface. It was to him, a place of peace and solitude especially at times like this when the airship was slowly moving though a thick field of white cumulus clouds. In the confines of his helmet of his EVA suit there was little sound. Not even the flow of air across the many iridescent blue solar panels which powered the Orion's batteries troubled him. He had clipped his safety line to one of the many long metal rods that ran between the banks of solar panels which formed a huge grid network designed for just such a purpose. There had been an indication on the main panel in the battery room that this area of the solar panels was only delivering about 30% of its potential, so he was now near the portside tail of the airship checking the output of the panels individually with his multimeter to find the offending panel or connection.

Suddenly, without warning the airship lifted up throwing the kneeling scientist flat onto his face, his body painfully hitting one of the metal safety rails as he slid across the slight curvature of the hull until his safety line went taut arresting his motion.

Down in the forward control cabin, second officer Heather Conrad indeed found that there was something wrong. She had fallen at the bottom of the small stairway which went down to the control cabin but quickly picked herself up. Rushing down the narrow companionway towards the cockpit, she noticed that the door to the radio room was wide open. There was not supposed to be anyone on duty and she had seen the radio operator, Fred Nicholls in the flight cabin before the final emergency alarm. She took a quick look into the small room and saw that the two radios which the Orion carried were both smashed. Rushing on to the cockpit, she found both pilots slumped forward in their seats, a neat bullet hole in the back of their heads. In front of them she saw to her horror, that the control panel and computer screens had all be smashed. Suddenly the airship leapt upwards as the safety capsule was ejected. Thrown off her feet, her head hit the edge of one of the control surfaces knocking her unconscious.

High above and to the stern of the airship, Paul Sinclair struggled to untangle himself from his safety line which had saved him from sliding off the curved hull. Half crawling, he began to haul himself back up the long safety line to where he had been testing the solar array before the airship had suddenly leaped upwards. Finally, he made it to the security of the long safety rod which was fastened to the hull. He wrapped his arm around it whilst he recovered his breath and composure. He lifted up the air-tight visor of his helmet and looked down at his old Pathfinder watch; the one his father had given him for Christmas those many years ago. The solar-powered watch not only gave an accurate time but also the current air temperature, pressure, compass direction and altitude. He was startled to see that the airship was well over its scheduled maximum altitude of two thousand metres, closer to three and getting higher.

Off to his side and further forward, he noticed a figure emerge from another one of the hooded access hatches about fifty metres away. It was also wearing an EVA suit and was attaching itself to a safety rod. Help would be greatly appreciated now.

There was no help there! Sinclair watched as though in slow motion as the figure raised what looked to be a firearm and take deliberate aim. He did not hear the shot but a long tear suddenly appeared in the flexible solar panel just in front of his face. He did not fully understand what was happening nor who it was who wanted to kill him. His only thought now was to escape. By chance, the rapid upward motion of the Orion had brought it up into the level of the cumulus clouds which had been previously drifting above. Now was his chance! He threw caution to the wind and unclipped his safely line and began to edge slowly along the safety rod away from his attacker and down the steep curvature of the hull towards the stern and the huge tailplane of the airship. He knew that near the base of each tailplane there was a maintenance hatchway to allow access to them. This is where he would make his escape into the interior of the hull. With his feet on the surface of the nearly horizontal tailplane, Sinclair was able to move from one vertical safety rod to another until he came to the maintenance hatch. Unsecuring the four latches which held the marine-type door closed, he opened it and crawled onto the small metal platform inside the hull. He had never really noticed it before, but unlike most of the framework of the Orion, the access ladders, narrow footways and safety platforms were all made of a shiny, grey metal; Duralumin.

Sinclair looked around from his small metal perch at the vast interior of the airship illuminated by the faint red glow of the emergency lighting running along the rails of the footway below. The huge, bulbous gas bags which gave the Orion its lift only made the scene more macabre and looking more like something out of Dante's *Inferno*.

No time to waste. His attacker may have followed him down to the tailplane. He turned around grasping the small, metal rail of the ladder which took him down about thirty metres to the footway which ran along this side of the airship. There were two of these major thoroughfares which ran on either side within the interior of the hull; both situated above the accommodation sections of the main deck. The riggers in their humorous way had christened these walkways Pitt Street and George Street after the two main thoroughfares which ran parallel, north to south, through the CBD of Sydney on the eastern coastline. Getting his bearings, he realised that he was climbing down to George Street on the port side of the airship.

There was little choice for escaping here. He was already at the stern of the airship and so he ran forward along the railed metal walkway, trying to remember where he could find a place to hide. He then suddenly put the past few minutes together and realised to his shock that he and his attacker may be the only two people onboard. It was obvious to him now that the safety capsule had ejected taking the guests and possibly all of the crew with it. There would be no one to help him and no where he could go. Except the hanger and cargo bay. There was still the Mini Orion, the small, electric powered light aircraft and the emergency parachutes. He had never felt the need to be trained in either flying or parachuting but now the latter seemed the best option for escape.

He had left his visor in the up position to give him a clearer idea of his escape route and noted that it was becoming more difficult to breathe. Suddenly there was a sharp, metallic 'ping' near his hand on the rail as a bullet ricocheted off it and splintered one of the bamboo stanchions nearby. Sinclair looked up and saw the figure in its EVA suit climbing down another access ladder from a more central hull hatchway some way forward. The figure now passed his arm through one of the ladder's rungs to get a better grip and to remove the silencer which had been attached to his pistol. He took off his EVA helmet to reveal the handsome dark features of Troy Jaeger, the head of security. Sinclair was confused so he cupped his hands together and yelled up at the other man:

"Don't shoot, Jaeger! It's me, Paul Sinclair, I'm no saboteur!" he said, pushing his visor higher up to expose all of his face.

Jaeger tightened his grip on the ladder and looked down at the other man and yelled:

"You boffins are all the same. Pretty stupid when it comes to reality! You couldn't sabotage a paper aeroplane. You should leave such things to the experts. After I get rid of you, this blimp is going to go up in flames and I'll parachute out into a million soft bucks in my bank account."

With that, Jaeger put both arms through the rung of his ladder to take a better, two-handed aim at the other man standing below. It was a long shot for a pistol, but Jaeger had often hit his man or target at that distance.

Sinclair looked about and saw that there was a smaller access ladder a few metres in front of him. If he could just make it before Jaeger took his shot, he may be able to get further down into the hull and closer to the cargo bay. The shot, when it came, was loud in the cavernous interior of the hull and it missed Sinclair by centimetres as he threw his body down onto the walkway. Luckily Jaeger had not decided to take another shot but was now climbing down his ladder to reach the walkway. Sinclair climbed over its rail and started to descend the smaller ladder. "Where did it go?" he thought.

It finished on top of an internal cabin roof near a small hatch. Opening it, he saw that he was in the roof of a familiar corridor, the one which led to the battery room where he had spent most of his working hours onboard. In the other direction there would be nothing but the main deck and the hangar. Not a good place to be when being hunted by an experienced gunman. He climbed down the small rungs set into the wall and jumped the last metre onto the metal floor of the passageway. He then unclipped his small tool bag from his belt and threw it down the passageway in the direction of the hangar hoping that Jaeger would see it and think that his prey had taken the obvious way out towards the front of the airship. Instead of going in that direction, Sinclair turned and ran along the passageway to the battery room further towards the stern.

The battery room was located in the lower section of the Orion amidships. It was a broad low ceilinged space which ran from one side of the airship to the other. It could only be accessed by the hatchways opening from the service passageways which ran along each side of the hull. These were kept closed at all times. Sinclair usually worked there on a daily basis so he knew the layout of the battery room. Without thinking, he quickly turned its single metal wheel, which was in the centre of the heavy bamboo door and entered. A single red lamp showed the long shelves of lithium-tungsten batteries which helped to power the Orion when the solar arrays where only delivering minimal power. These were held in racks running down both sides of the central aisle. At the far end, he knew that there was another hatchway leading out and back into another passageway but this would probably only prolong the hunt.

He closed the door to the battery room tightly and looked around for a suitable weapon in case Jaeger did not fall for his rouse of throwing his tool kit down the passageway. At a short distance down the central aisle of the battery room were maintenance racks of empty spare cells, lengths of connecting cables and large plastic, 20 litre containers of alkaline electrolyte which could be used to replenish the empty cells which could then be slotted into any defective battery. On the wall near the door was a fire extinguisher and a fire axe. Neither appealed to Sinclair as an effective weapon. The extinguisher was of the carbon dioxide type and would probably only annoy Jaeger if it was sprayed at him; the axe also would be useless against a trained assassin like Jaeger. Only an idiot would take an axe to a gunfight!

Sinclair sat down on the cold metal surface of the central aisle and tried to think. As a young boy at school, he had always been able to avoid or prevent being bullied by using his intelligence. He looked around again at his familiar surroundings and suddenly found the weapon he had been looking for – electricity.

The Orion's motors ran on relatively low voltage so as not to allow for electrical discharges, but to provide enough power to them, the amount of current, or amperage, had to be high. It was the amount of current, rather than the voltage which caused injury and death in electrocutions. Moreover, the metal structure of the walkway and that of the door locking wheel would be ideal terminals for an electric circuit.

Sinclair got up and found the one of the emergency isolating switches which he often had to switch to the off position whenever he removed or replaced cells within that bank of batteries. Running down to the storage shelves at the end of the room, he grabbed a large container of electrolyte and several of the power cables. He rushed back to the isolated batteries and quickly connected the main terminals, which were at the end of the entire bank to two of the long cables. In just this small bank of batteries, there would be more than enough electrical current to be lethal. The textbooks all said that anything over 200 milliamperes was dangerous, a figure which he thought was impossibly small. This bank of batteries would deliver more than one full ampere at their standard low voltage. He connected the bulldog clips of the electrical cables to the inside metal locking wheel of the door and to the edge of metal walkway. All he needed was to ensure that the current would pass between the two terminals. To do this, he would have to pour the electrolyte onto the walkway outside of the door and hope that Jaeger would not see the pool of conducting liquid in the low emergency lighting. He also hoped that the boots which were worn with the rest of the EVA suits would also assist in the conducting process. These boots were made of felt to prevent damage to the solar arrays out on the hull and to also provide some grip. There had been some complaints from the riggers that in wet weather, they tended to fill with water; a feature which was no problem for their intended purpose but a discomfort for their wearer.

Sinclair opened the door to the battery room and poured a liberal amount of electrolyte right up to the door and for a couple of metres beyond, completely emptying the large, plastic container. He was just in time as he saw Jaeger drop down from the roof hatch onto the walkway. Jaeger landed facing the battery room and saw Sinclair face in the dim, red light. "Got you!" Jaeger thought.

Sinclair slammed the door shut and turned the locking wheel to its full lock, knowing that this would slow him down. He rushed over to the bank of isolating switch ready to activate the bank of batteries now connected to the door lock and the walkway. But first, he placed the large, empty electrolyte container and stood on it hoping that it would insulate him from any current within the walkway. He saw the locking wheel of the door slowly turning and he threw the isolating switch to its on position.

7.

Second officer Heather Conrad regained consciousness and realised that apart from the lump on her head, she was having difficulties breathing. Standing up, she looked out of the forward cabin windows and saw a wide expanse of fluffy white. She realised then that the Orion was well above the cumulus clouds which she knew at the pre-flight met report should have a base of about ten thousand feet – a little over three thousand metres. It was no wonder that she was having difficulties breathing as the airship was probably well above four thousand feet above sea level and still rising. She needed help. Walking back to the radio room, she found to her relief that the PA system was untouched. Throwing the send switch, she spoke as calmly as she could. Her heart beating rapidly with the low oxygen level and her distress:

"Hello. Is anyone out there onboard? This is second officer Heather Conrad in the control cabin. If you can hear me, please come to the control cabin. I need some help.

There was not the bright flash and crackle of high voltage electricity when Paul Sinclair threw the isolating switch to on. Only a loud, piercing scream and the rancid smell of burnt flesh. He waited for a short while and leant over from his makeshift insulated platform and turned off the isolation switch. Carefully he reached down and touched the metal surface of the walkway with his knuckle knowing from his training and experience that the hand often closed around objects carrying electrical current. No reaction. No shock.

Stepping down off the large plastic container, he cautiously went to the door of the battery room and listened with his ear to its wooden panel. No sound of movement, voice or breathing. Slowly he turned the central locking wheel of the door until it unlatched and pushed outwards. There was some resistance so he put his shoulder to the door and pushed with all of his strength. The door slowly moved open in small amounts leaving just enough room for his slim body to pass through. He carefully looked around the edge of the door not knowing whether or not Jaeger was still alive and up to some trick. No! Jaeger's body lay partly across the bottom of the door, his arm still upraised and his burnt fingers wrapped around the central locking wheel. He was dead.

Sinclair pushed out through the door and past the body. "Electrocution was a bad way to die," he thought, but he had little remorse for the man who had sought his own death and who had hunted him throughout the Orion. Standing on the walkway looking at Jaeger's body, Sinclair was suddenly woken from his thoughts about death by the crackle of the loudspeaker which was on the bulkhead near the battery room door.

He recognised Heather Conrad's tearful voice and heard her plea for help. He wasn't an empathetic man, but her plea gave him a sudden sense of joy and relief that here was someone who could help get him to safety. He ran down the walkway towards the forward part of the airship. He knew that the usual way through the flight cabin would be impossible because it no longer existed, so he would have to go to the main deck and through one of the small service hatchways which led from the hangar to the narrow companionway used by off duty crew going between the control cabin and their quarters above the battery room.

It took only a few minutes to reach the small ladder which went down into the rear of the control cabin. He found the second officer still at the desk in the radio room slumped over the microphone of the PA system. He had wondered why his exertions against Jaeger had been slow and difficult to perform. He realised then that the Orion was still rising and so now they would be soon above the level of normal breathing. He also had not worried about removing the helmet from his EVA suit but had foolishly kept its airtight visor up. He quickly removed the helmet and placed it over the head of the unconscious woman. With the flow of fresh oxygen she stirred, slowly sat up and looked around.

"Paul?" she said, her eyes beginning to focus on the person standing over her.

"Sorry, Heather. My turn for some air now." He removed the helmet from her and replaced it over his head, took several deep breaths and then gave it back.

She also took several deep breaths then returned the helmet to her benefactor:

"In the cockpit," she said gasping for extra air which was not there "the emergency oxygen masks have dropped down. We can breathe through those." Quickly they both left the radio room and ran up the short corridor to the cockpit where Sinclair was shocked to find the two pilots still slumped in their seats. Heather passed him a mask whilst she attached one to her own face. She quickly explained what she had done after seeing Jaeger talking to Sir Ewan and seeing the startled look on his face.

"I was too late." She looked sadly at Sinclair gesturing towards the wrecked console. "The saboteur had been here well before Jaeger had found this mess."

"You could not have done anything because it was Jaeger who was the saboteur all along. It was he who killed Dawson back at the base. Dawson probably found his boss sending the signal to his cronies outside. If you had got here any sooner, you would be like poor captain Eichner and first officer Helmuth Zabel. Can you still fly this thing?"

The second officer was the third pilot onboard the Orion. She now looked around the cabin with new hope. With Sinclair's help, she carefully unbuckled the bodies of the two dead pilots and dragged them to radio room where they lay them on the floor and covered them with a fire blanket.

"Captain Eichner was a pilot of the old school" she said, looking down at the bodies. "He relished the use of computer controls and all of our electronic navigation and such but he always believed that an aircraft should also be able to be flown by – what's the expression? – by the seat of one's pants."

He turned around and looked at Sinclair and pointed to a broad, wooden locker near the rear portside part of the cabin.

"Can you reach that locker?" she said, opening another compartment in a centre console behind the pilots' seats. This had doors which swung right open and around the sides of the console revealing a metal rod with two flanges on either side.

Sinclair took several deep breaths and left his oxygen mask to open the locker. In it he found a spoked metal wheel latched upright against the locker's rear wall. It was similar to a small ship's wheel which he had often seen on small motor boats. He wrenched it from its supports and brought it over to the second officer who pushed it firmly onto the metal rod of the small central console.

"Right! Now we have steerage! Next we must vent some of the gas in the ballonette to reduce our altitude." Saying that she too dropped her mask and went over to a metal wheel which was jutting out from a tube which ran up into the hull of the airship. "This is the way the old Zeppelin commanders did it but I have no way of knowing our altitude as the computer screens and our manual altimeter have both been smashed."

"Got it covered!" said Sinclair taking off his Pathfinder watch which was still set at altimeter mode. He showed it in triumph to Heather and placed it on top of the small console above the new airship's wheel. "Not overly accurate but it will work. There is also a compass mode too if we need it."

"We'll need it. Our GPS and analogue compass are both wrecked but they are useless without power to our engines."

Sinclair touched the side of his nose with his finger and gave Heather a wink. "Leave it to the boffin. Remember that I am the grand high poohbah of electricity on this vessel. I can override the emergency shutoff system from the switch room up near the main deck. I will have to go back up the staff ladder but it won't take long. How much power do you want?"

"Half speed should be enough. I'll vent the gas until we get to about two thousand feet and head east and then we will have to think of what to do next. There are only about two hours of daylight left and I don't know if I can fly her in the dark to get back to base."

Sinclair smiled at her innocence and put his EVA helmet back on. "Back in a jiffy. Don't hit anything," he joked.

Second officer Heather Conrad heard the quiet hum of the nearest two ducted electric fan motors and the main lights come back on and felt reassured. She now had full control of the airship. All that was needed was to get somewhere before the sun set. There was no hope in returning to base and no radio to call for help and all cell phones had been left at the base for security purposes – Sir Ewan was paranoid, he did not even trust his aircrew.

When Sinclair returned, she explained both the good news about her ability to fly the stricken airship and the bad news that they would not make it back to base nor could they radio for help. Sinclair thought for a moment.

"What about the Mini Orion? She's got a radio – only short range, but we might be able to raise someone locally."

"Great idea, Paul. Can you do it, please? I would like to get the Orion down a bit lower and then adjust our direction eastward. How do you do that with your wonderful watch?"

Sinclair showed her the small black buttons on his Pathfinder watch which would toggle the mode between altimeter and compass. With a wave of his hand, he climbed back up the ladder and headed towards the hangar. Running along the metal walkway and down the service ladder into the hangar, Sinclair walked carefully across the closed circular hatch in the floor of the Orion. He climbed into the small aircraft and flicked on all of the switches. He had no training as a pilot but he had a little understanding of the radio and how it worked. He found the UHF radio and was comforted that it had power. He switched the frequency knob to Channel 5 at 476.5250 MHZ and pressed the handset to begin to send.

"Mayday. Mayday. This is the airship Orion. Come in anyone. Over." Nothing.

He repeated this several times; each time letting go of the send button and listening carefully to the small loudspeaker in the roof above him. Nothing.

He tried again and listened. After what seemed to be an eternity there was a crackling sound and a faint, disjointed voice came from the loud speaker.

"Orion! You're…an…airship?…Over?"

Heartened, Sinclair repeated his distress call and added:

"Yes! Whoever you are I am mighty glad to hear you. We are in distress and are trying to land. Can you help? Over!" He gave the overall dimensions of the delta-wing airship and the fact that it could softly land anywhere that had that space.

"Yeah, mate! " The voice now came in stronger as the sender had obviously increased his power output. "You've got the dispatcher at the Cobar Excelsior Copper Mine here. I'm used to controlling dirty big trucks not airships but I'll do me best. We've got a dirty big open cut pit which could fit several of you in. What do you need? Over!"

"Probably a lot of lighting and some people to hold us down as we land. Can you do that? Over!"

"No problem, sport. We're a mine, see. We work 24/7 and have enough portable floodlights to light up the Sydney Cricket ground. Also, we have plenty of guys and some dirty big machines which we could use to anchor yer balloon. Where are ya? Over!"

"Great! At last position we were heading east not far from the Menindee Lakes but I think that we have drifted a little so I am not sure of our exact position. We have regained control and will bring her down to about two thousand metres. Over!"

"Listen mate! The wind here has been blowing from the north so you probably went a little to the south. Turn her due north and look for the A32 – the Barrier Highway. It's the only straight line you'll see going between us and Broken Hill out west. Find her and turn east and follow it. You are probably between Wilcannia and Cobar so you can't miss us. We're a dirty big open cut like I said, so we'll look like a big bullseye from the air. Just keep her low. OK? Over!"

"Thanks friend. I let the pilot know and we will try to get there before dark. Thanks for your help. See you later. Over"

"Yeah! Cheers mate. I'll get the lads ready and we'll see ya soon. Out!"

Sinclair raced back to the control cabin to give pilot Heather the good news and instructions about how to find the mine. Carefully, she turned the Orion to the north according to Sinclair's watch. Sinclair, optimistic as usual took a pair of binoculars and searched the land in front of the airship for the highway. The sun had almost set when a long ribbon of tarmac could be seen stretching diagonally across their front; the afternoon sun giving it a healthy golden glow. Heather turned the wheel to bring the airship over the highway and asked Sinclair to vent more gas to get lower.

"I'll take her down to about two hundred metres. There's nothing much on these plains anywhere near that height and we can follow the lights of traffic if it gets dark."

From this higher altitude, Sinclair could see the lights of several vehicles well-spaced along the highway. "Hardly a peak hour, but it will do," he thought.

It would only be about an hour when they could see a bright corona of light coming up from the plain just north and west of a cluster of many smaller lights that would be the mining town of Cobar famous for its vast deposits of copper which had been found north of the town in recent years invigorating the entire economy.

"Well! Our dispatcher friend was certainly right about the city lights! Sinclair said as he refocussed the binoculars onto a large ring of bright industrial floodlights on their tractor stands which circled a huge open cut pit. The sides of the pit went down progressively smaller as the road benches reached the bottom. This was now well lit from another ring of floodlights situated halfway up the pit. The entire scene looked like something out of a science fiction movie with the Orion now playing the role of the huge alien mothership.

"You had better go back to the switch room, Paul and get ready to stop the motors." Heather said. Normally, the ducted fan motors could be rotated to help the descent or ascent of the airship or even turned completely around to slow and stop her. Unfortunately, the rotation mechanism had been damaged along with the automatic landing controls. They would have to bring the airship down by the old-fashioned method of coming over the landing strip and venting gas to descend. If they could get low enough, the long handling ropes which Sinclair had been able to throw out from the sides of the hull, could be grabbed by those on the ground to guide the unpowered airship to a good landing place. This relied on Sinclair's stopping the motors at the exact minute so that the airship would slow its drift and be exactly over the huge bullseye of the mine. To do this, they would communicate on the internal telephone system which luckily had not been damaged. Heather would have to use her experience and flight training to be able to estimate the wind direction and rate of drift of the airship.

"Now!" came Heather's voice over the earpiece of the telephone and Sinclair in the switch room cut power to all of the engines. In the cockpit, Heather had quickly left the pilot's seat and rotated the wheel to vent as much air as possible so that the giant airship would sink as fast as possible into the pit.

Below, the handling ropes snaked down across the road benches of the mine and were grabbed by the large number of miners, many of whom had come from the town along with other volunteers. Soon there was a long line of human bodies on the trailing ends of the handling lines and the Orion was being slowly hauled down. This was helped by winches on two of the huge 20 tonne dump trucks to which one of the foremen had attached the fore and aft handling lines. The Orion's ventral skids slowly touched ground. The Orion had finally landed.

Epilogue

The safety capsule came down as gently as predicted nor far from the road which leads to the town of Ivanhoe about fifty kilometres away. Just before landing on the red-brown plain covered in low scrub, airbags were opened from their compartments on the base of the capsule and these enabled it to settle softly on the small trees which were flattened by its weight. The side doors of the capsule were similar to those of aircraft and opened with a loud pop as their explosive bolts fired. A long rubber and canvas chute opened out to form a long slide to the ground down which the passengers exited. Ted Campbell, ever practical, organised some of the crew to gather firewood and soon had a good fire going under a copse of trees at some distance from the capsule.

In Canberra, the nation's capital some 620 kilometres to the southeast, the signal from the Orion capsule's Emergency Position Indicating Radio Beacon (EPIRB), had been picked up by the Cospas-Sarsat 12 international search and rescue satellite and relayed to the Australian Joint Rescue Coordination Centre (JRCC) there. At first the location seemed to be a strange one for an emergency beacon normally fitted to ships, but once its registration had been verified as belonging to the airship Orion, a call was put out to the local State Emergency Service (SES) at Ivanhoe. The landing of the capsule however had already been observed by a local grazier rounding up some cattle and so it was not long before a 4WD emergency truck arrived on the scene. Having ascertained that all on board the capsule were in good health, local property owners readily volunteered to come out to the crash site and take all onboard back to the town.

Meanwhile some time much later, in the depths of the open cut mine near Cobar, Heather Conrad and Paul Sinclair had been taken up to the mine manager's office amongst a group of cheering miners and treated to warm food and plenty of alcohol which, of course was forbidden on the mine site.

By now, the media had got wind of the voyage of the Orion, thanks to the young reporter from the Herald who had convinced the local postmaster to open after hours and transmit his story back to his newspaper by Scanmail. It was broadcasted on local television and thus seen by Heather and Paul at the mine site whilst awaiting transportation to nearby Cobar. It was not long before Sir Ewan Hunter had telephoned his headquarters in Sydney to arrange for local buses to take all of the passengers and crew of the Orion back to a luxury hotel in the city for some R & R and a debrief of the crew. On the way, Heather and Paul were picked up at the mining company's office in Cobar. The dispatcher and the mine staff and volunteers who had facilitated the landing of the Orion were all rewarded with complementary flights to local holiday destinations of their choice by Hunter Aviation.

Heather Conrad was given a well-deserved promotion to first officer and Paul Sinclair was given leave to take up the short-term but prestigious scholarship to the American university which he had been previously denied. Sir Ewan had confidence that the young scientist's experiences on board the Orion would not dampen his enthusiasm for assisting with the development of its sister ships, both cargo and passenger designations. It had been an exciting few days, but the Orion had proven by rather dramatic means that a dirigible airship was both an efficient and safe way of travelling.

DOWNLOAD

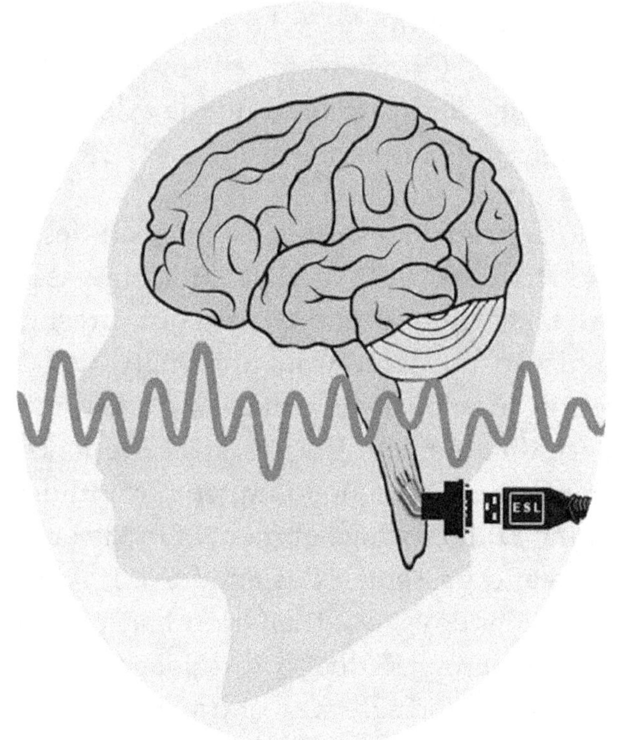

1.

There was something strange about Emiliano. Even his parents had problems understanding his behaviour. After all, there had been nothing unusual at his birth. In fact, the family obstetrician was very happy about the delivery and gave an excellent prognosis for the new baby. The family's general neurosurgeon, Doctor Blimber, had proudly stated that all of the brain scans and electroencephalograph readings had shown a much higher than average neurone count and synapse frequency rate.

His doting parents, Muriel and Stanley had retired to suburban affluence years ago; Muriel had been an eNurse at the local hospital and had spent most of her career trying to avoid the flashing red lights and buzzers coming from the Life Support and Repair Capsules of her patients, whilst Stanley had made a fortune trading in cryptocurrency back in the 2040's. Now, all of their spare time, when they were not 'doing coffee and eChat' with their many like-minded friends on their socially Superior A-Network, was devoted to young Emiliano. Well, that was in actual fact very little time, but they made sure that he had plenty of eGames at home and even a robotic dog to play with. Their only major concern was that young Emiliano had not achieved the rotund body shape like most children of his age. This was probably because he ate very little, especially the large supersized eBurgers which formed the staple diet of the Montalban family these were delivered by Hoverbot drone directly from the local eBurger outlet.

"Why don't you like your eBurgers?" Stanley Montalban would angrily pester his young son when he got older. "They won't kill you!"

Thus, young Emiliano grew up like most of such privileged children in the City and so looked forward to going to eSchool and receiving his First Implant.

His parents told him that this would be a great event; it would be streamed, of course, and his many friends on Fritface would all give him a Like. At home, the few close family members who were invited to the small party in the Montalban's supersized residence, would all be involved in young Emiliano's coming of eAge, which made his supersized parents, Muriel and Stanley very happy, they would immediately post the event on their account on Fritface.

It was a great time to be alive in any of the Greater Networked Cities of the GNCs as they were internationally called. There was now uniformity and social harmony throughout the digitised world. Mind you – there were still many pockets of depressed civilisation, if you could call it that - where the Network was poorly received or even non-existent. The poor people in these places did not have the benefit of modern eScience nor of connected social interaction and had to contend with the grime and odour of face-to-face contact.

Things had developed rapidly in the second half of the Twenty-first Century ever since Schwartzberg and Blohnmann had discovered that the human brain could be modified by using downloaded electrical impulses for which they had received the 2030 Nobel Prize in medicine. Now all of the required knowledge, skills and attitudes of a previously disjointed and cumbersome worldwide education system could be downloaded directly into the brain stem and into the thalamus – that central switchboard which helps in the regulation of the neural pathways of the brain.

These two worthies had discovered their Neural Receptance, as they had called the complex interaction between electrical brain stimulation and learning, from their separate studies on neurological stimulation on mental patients and paraplegics. There was nothing new about electronic brain stimulation (EBS) and this branch of psychomedicine had progressed rapidly since Luigi Galvani had discovered accidentally that the muscles of the legs of frogs could be excited by the new electricity way back in 1780. The idea had rapidly caught on and so by the end of the nineteenth century and early twentieth century, medicos and researchers were busily applying electrical stimuli to their patients to cure all sorts of illness and defects from baldness to epilepsy.

The real breakthrough came in the second half of the twentieth century with the work of such researchers as Hess, Delgado and Penfold who had used long-term or chronic electrode implants directly into parts of the brains of their patients to stimulate emotions or physical movement. These studies went a long way in the control and improvement of mental illnesses and impaired motor body ability.

It was in 2023 that Doctor Bernard Schwartzberg, the renowned Swiss neurosurgeon, discovered that neurons – brain cells - could be regenerated and modified by direct electrical stimulation which he found had restored memory in patients with Alzheimer's disease. This was followed independently by the work of Professor Alice Blohnmann, the Australian Neurosurgeon and Musician who had found that the frequency of electrical stimuli could produce a corresponding resonance in synapse transmission and improved function of neurotransmitters. This enabled her to program, as it were, the parts of the brain responsible for various mental functions. This enabled the forgotten memories to be retaught. She called this ability Neural Encoding. This too, had been another example of serendipity, when she had discovered that one of her brain-damaged patients, who had also been a noted clarinet player, had recovered his knowledge of how to play the note A above middle C when the stimulus frequency of 440 Hertz was electrically encoded directly into his brain.

Following their award of the 2030 Nobel Prize for Medicine, Schwartzberg and Blohnmann collaborated and began research into the new field of Electrically Stimulated Learning (ESL) using rats and maze learning. Hoffer and Smith took the concept of these studies to new heights when they applied ESL to human volunteers in mental institutions and prisons. Their experiments continued despite a great hue and cry from a minority of the general public who still cared about old-fashioned sentiments and morals and thought that tinkering with the human brain was unnatural. Which it was.

Hoffer and Smith also found that direct downloads of new information in rats could only be done at certain times in their mental development. Thus, it was impossible to download information that required an adult's mature brain function to a young rat. Furthermore, it was found that human volunteers only retained new, downloaded information if they had learned previous steps required to understand this new learning. To understand this concept, Hoffer and Smith fell back on the early work of the twentieth century Swiss psychologist Jean Piaget who had stated that intelligence developed in a series of stages that are related to age and are progressive because one stage must be accomplished before the next can occur. It was their Neo-Piagetian view that specific ESL content could only be applied when the subject was ready for it and to achieve maximum learning in any area, data had to be downloaded progressively in developmental stages.

Their work had come to the attention of Erez Andersen, the multi-trillionaire owner of Cyber Ware, that multinational software monopoly which had long since taken over most of the billionaires who had owned the software and internet companies of the early part of the twenty-first century. His researchers had no trouble in finding many willing young volunteers whose families were paid huge amounts for their services. The noted neurosurgeon and employee of Cyber Ware, Doctor Brace Willard, had invented a multi-channel electrode system which could be surgically inserted directly to the thalamus of the brain which would then channel the various frequencies and amplitudes of signal input to the most appropriate parts of the brain. He and his team soon discovered that specific knowledge would be neurally encoded and directed into the hippocampus, the neocortex and the amygdala – those parts of the brain responsible for explicit memory. Later, when experimenting with members of the boxing fraternity, who had suffered brain damage in the boxing ring, they had found that neurally encoded stimulation of the basal ganglia and cerebellum of the brain could restored their lost motor skills in that sport although little else.

The final chapter in the development of eLearning as it became popularly known, came in 2052 with the work of Doctor Chuck Nǎo of Cyber Ware's Public Relations. When investigating some of the early researches into human emotions and direct electrical stimulation of the brain, he had found that very specific emotions, interests and indeed attitudes, both positive and negative, could also be programmed and implanted into the limbic system. The limbic system is that group of interconnected structures located deep within the brain which is responsible for behavioural and emotional responses.

Soon Cyber Ware was developing alternative software in their eEducation Division for schools and advocating the use of direct download of information into the brains of students. At first, the general public of the developed nations of the Greater Networked Cities were sceptical of such a radical treatment of the educational process. After all, such traditional teaching methods had been tried and tested since the days of Plato and the ancient Greeks. However, some aggressive politicians who wished to be seen to be progressive and so regain their seats at the next election, had argued that such old-fashioned systems of education took up large amounts of national budgets, mostly due to the exorbitant salaries of teachers, which could be better spent on armaments and national defence.

Thus, the first eSchool opened in Washington D.C. naturally enough, as this was seen as one of the leading education centres of the 'free world' of the Greater Networked Cities. There was no shortage of cashed-up parents who wanted their five-year-olds to be leaders of a future eSociety, leading the world in all of the Arts and Sciences. There also was no shortage of neurosurgeons who looked towards the next awards of the Nobel Prize in Medicine wishing to demonstrate their surgical skills.

Of course, there were bound to be some failures, but these were quickly hushed up by the various media outlets, all owned or directly influenced by Erez Andersen and Cyber Ware. What was published loud and clear in all of the eJournals and SurroundTV channels were the great successes of the new system. They extolled the talents of various five-year-old members of eSchool Washington 0001 who were now able to do astounding things as a result of their new eLearning. Young virtuosi on a range of musical instruments and children who could recite the entire Declaration of Independence and similar astounding feats soon hit the screens of all of the Greater Networked Cities.

Even in those countries which could not claim 'free world' allegiance soon started their own eEducation systems and obedient parents were instructed to take their precious One-child to receive their First Implant. Naturally the Russian Democratic Federation claimed that the entire process had been invented by them in the previous year and the Unified Chinese People's Popular Democracy loudly pointed out that the basic idea could be traced back to the Tung Dynasty. In fact, aspects of their systems and computer software bore great similarities to that of Cyber Ware and it was often suggested by the usual conspiracy 'Investigative Journalists' on SurroundTV that such programs and techniques were the result of cyber espionage and theft. Cyber Ware and most 'free world' governments gave little credence to such unsubstantiated assertions, as both of these countries had been successfully commercially saturated with legitimate software along with other profitable cultural necessities such as 'take-away' mass food market. EBurgers were a very popular line both inside and outside of the 'free world'.

Thus, First Implant celebrations soon became, for social and propaganda reasons, the first major coming-of-age for young children in developed countries and was thus celebrated worldwide with as much pomp and circumstance as the family could afford.

In the Montalban Family supersized residence, the First Implant celebration for young Emiliano had been a multimedia spectacular. Muriel and Stanley Montalban had hired the best production team in the City to beam out this grand event to all of their many friends on their extensive eChat channel on their Superior A-Network and on their Fritface account. A few very close relatives had taken the trouble to leave their screens and come over to the Montalban supersized residence to act as 'social background' and to enjoy the food and drink lavishly supplied by the local eBurger outlet. Only grandfather Adam had refused to stay for the party because it was said by Stanley that he still lived in the past and cared little for such 'social' media events. However, he did love his little grandson and stayed long enough to wish the small boy happiness and console him about his sore head.

So after having wished young Emiliano a happy First Implant with a gentle kiss on the child's aching forehead, he had returned to his home for a quiet night and with one of his antique books which he kept hidden away in an old chest in his attic. The party was now in full swing online with the full display of joy and happiness, electronically supplemented by artificial laughter and party background sounds with music. Every one of the background relatives and the Montalban parents were seen to be having much fun and the Likes came freely from their Fritface screen. Little Emiliano was the only one not participating in the happy event; he sat quietly in the corner away from the cameras holding his robotic dog and rubbing the painful back of his neck and its new small metal input socket.

2.

To the Montalban family, little Emiliano's early childhood seemed quite normal, although father Stanley thought that it was slightly unusual for his little boy to prefer playing eGames and simulations which required only one participant rather than to engage actively in online socialisation with other children of his age. Stanley had even opened a Fritface account for the boy, but little Emiliano seemed totally disinterested and liked playing outside with his robotic dog, Edison instead.

Other than this tendency to keep to himself, Emiliano seemed just as happy and clever as most of the children of the Montalban' eChat group. There was nothing much of the outside world which troubled the Montalbans; the local media saw to that by simply keeping all news items confined to sports events and the scandals of media personalities.

It was at the start of February in the next year, when the young Emiliano was dressed in his best clothes, given a small food eCard and taken by a weeping Mrs Montalban out to the road in front of their supersize mansion to wait for the big yellow autoBus which was to take him to his first day at eSchool (Intro). Mrs. Montalban gave her son a kiss on top of his head and with a tear in her eye, waddled back to her front door, leaving little Emiliano on the kerb to wait by himself for the big Yellow autoBus.

Naturally, the local autoBus had been recently programmed at the Ministry of Auto Transport to stop at the Montalban's supersized residence at precisely 8:35 am every school day and convey the new scholar to his eSchool several klicks away. Mrs Montalban, meanwhile had returned to her daily morning program on SurroundTV to find out what were the startling new Virtual Reality shows for the coming year.

Eventually, at precisely 8:35, the big yellow autoBus stopped opposite the front gate of the Montalban's supersize residence and its doors opened. Emiliano climbed up the big steps with some apprehension; he wasn't reassured by the large, electronic image of a smiling mature lady with grey hair and glasses and the electronic voice saying:

"Welcome to our friends on our lovely bus which will take you to your very own sc.. sc.. sc.. school."

The fault in the audio and the lack of a human driving the bus did not reduce Emiliano's apprehension at all, as this was also his first time away from home.

He carefully moved up the aisle of the bus as its door slammed shut and its soundless, electronic motors slowly brought the vehicle up to its sedate standard speed. A few heads of the other occupants, mostly children of a variety of ages, were raised to look at the new arrival, but they were engrossed in the eGames and messages on their phones or eTablets. There were also a few adults sitting at the back of the bus looking rather self-conscious that they should be in an eSchool bus. They were eTechs and other human administrators who preferred to take the free bus than take their own cars off home charge.

Emiliano found a vacant seat and plugged his own eTablet into the charging socket and logged into his favourite game of Hermit Squirrel. He soon found that the consequences of arriving at his destination, like the other students on the autoBus, was soon mentally put aside.

Now Emiliano's doting parents had done their research before selecting an appropriate eSchool for their young son well before his 5+ Download. According to their Superior A-Network, eSchool Primary #4069 was one of the better eSchools in the City. It had been established well over one hundred years ago, in 1951 before the advent of Electrically Stimulated Learning (ESL), when all information had to be laboriously imparted from people called Teachers over a long period of time using only visual, verbal and other stimuli. Emiliano knew that grandfather Adam had been a Teacher and had probably attended such an archaic institution. At least in his final days before retirement, he had used computers and interactive programs as well as books to impart information to his students; or so he had often told his young grandson many times during one of his frequent visits to the Montalban household. Grandfather Adam had been very proud of his previous career despite its primitive methods and its often socially turbulent environment.

After a short time of slowly crawling along its GPS-fixed route through the dormitory suburbs, the autoBus arrived at eSchool Primary #4069. Its double front doors opened slowly and the dysfunctional electronic image of the smiling mature lady with grey hair and glasses wished the departing children to have a "hap…hap… happy d.. d.. d.. day!"

There was another smiling mature lady with grey hair and glasses – a real person this time – waiting for them at the school gate.

"Hello, children!" she said with a happy lilt in her voice. "Welcome to eSchool Primary #4069. Would all of the new students come with me, please?"

All of the other older occupants of the bus already knew where their classrooms were located and waddled off in different directions, their eyes and fingers still on the screens of their phones. The tired-looking eTechs, who had occupied the backseats of the autoBus, knew exactly where the staffroom and its coffee machines was located; it was always difficult for them to start the day at eSchool.

Emiliano and the other children of the recent 5+ Download followed the smiling mature lady with grey hair and glasses; some of his group actually put their phones away and looked around at their new surroundings. They were now walking down a long corridor which had well-trampled, faded linoleum on a wooden floor and very tall windows set high up on one side. Great beams of bright sunlight came through each window giving the dusty corridor a magical effect. Below the windows was a long row of wooden racks which the lady explained used to hold the heavy satchels and books of past students back before the days of eTablets.

"Now of course, you don't have to carry heavy books and other ancient things like pencils and crayons," she said with a sigh remembering her own schooldays from a distant past when she happily carried her special satchel with its many books, pencils and crayons. "Today we only need our eTablet - you all have it, I hope?" she said as an afterthought.

She carefully opened a door in the wall on the other side of the corridor to the big windows. This led into an airy room which had brightly coloured yellow walls and blue thick-pile round floor mats.

"Please sit down, children" she said with another smile and turned to a large SurroundTV screen which was mounted on the wall at the far end of the room. She turned it on with a remote handset and then walked towards the rear of the room. "Please pay attention, children. Our Principal, Mrs Hinder wishes to personally welcome you."

The screen lit up and the logo of eSchool Primary #4069 came onto the screen in two dimensions. It was a simple, round shield in yellow with a flaming red torch through which the numbers '4069' inscribed across the blue flame. There was a Latin motto below which stated *'Lumen Siccum'* and the significance of the dry light of learning escaped Emiliano and others who saw the badge. It was just the symbol for the school and nothing else as far as most were concerned.

Slowly, a 3D hologram of another smiling mature lady with grey hair and glasses appeared in the centre of the room in front of the screen. This apparently was the school's Principal, Mrs Hinder and Emiliano wondered if every person in eSchools had to meet such physical criteria as being mature with grey hair and glasses.

The firm but friendly voice carefully matched the image this time but came from speakers set further back in the room. The voice again welcomed them to eSchool Primary #4069 and hoped that here they would find many interesting things to do in putting real meaning to their recent 5+ Download and would have fun practicing their newly-acquired knowledge and skills. Each student would have their very own console and the school had plenty of eGames and simulations to expand their new knowledge and skills with both mental and physical interaction. Their very own eTech would be there for each class, of course, to help them understand the programs and to get all of the materials needed for the many computer-activated work tasks.

Of course, there were to be rules to follow. One could not simply rely on the Socially-responsible algorithm of the 5+ Download to ensure cooperation and personal responsibility the voice from the speakers at the back of the room said. There were only two eSchool rules: school must be a happy place; and no one had the right to interfere with another's education.

Emiliano was encouraged by these two simple rules. He had been warned by Grandfather Adam who had once told him tales of his own hard school days with pages of school rules dictating everything from how they wore their uniform – there were none at eSchool Primary #4069 – to where they were to eat their lunch. Later, he was to find however, that any variation from what the eTech and Mrs Hinder though was normal would be a breach of both of these school rules.

The hologram of the smiling mature lady with grey hair and glasses slowly faded with only the smile lingering to the end. This was much the same as Emiliano was later to read in one of Grandfather Adam's book about a Cheshire Cat.

The other smiling mature lady with grey hair and glasses who had brought them to the room now spoke up in the same firm but friendly voice which also seemed to be part of the eSchool human standard.

"Now, children" she said. "You have been allocated classes depending upon your post 5+ neurological assessment and I will now read out the names of children in our four new 5+ Intro classes.

She carefully read out the names in each class starting from Rodrigo Aaronson and ending with Jaime Ziegfeld, allocating each child to either of the Intro-1 or Intro-2 classes. Emiliano was to be in the Intro-1 class. As his neurological assessment to him had been just another plug-in by his General Neurosurgeon following his traumatic First Insertion, he had no feelings of superiority about being in the top graded class.

3.

Time went swiftly for Emiliano Montalban of Class Intro-1 at eSchool Primary #4069. Each day his mother would take him by the hand and waddle down to the side of the road in front of their supersized residence and see that he had his lunch eCard, eTablet and that he got on the autoBus for school. He knew the way to his classroom by now and so he would find his room at the end of the long corridor with its high windows on one side, through the brightly-coloured door and to his very own console where he would call up the notices for the day on the school's Fritface account.

Mrs. Elliot was always in the classroom early. She was the eTech for Intro-1 and unlike all of the ladies he had met so far, she was not a mature lady with grey hair and glasses; but she did smile a lot. Mrs. Gabriella Elliot was in fact only a little past what one might call her youth, but her hair was still black, well most of it, and it was always tied behind with a bright pink ribbon. She was always neatly dressed in some bright colour and Emiliano thought that she was the most wonderful person he had ever met.

Once every one of her class had arrived, she would sit them down in the middle of the room on the blue thick-pile round floor mats and call the roll. She did this in a most pleasant and personal manner with a smile and some simple acknowledgement of the child.

"Emiliano Montalban? Why, Emiliano! You are looking smart today! Is that a new eBook case you have?" she would say in her soft, melodious voice.

"Yes, Mam" or "Yes, Mrs. Elliot," would be the usual reply.

Once the daily tasks were reviewed from the Fritface page, which now appeared on the large SurroundTV screen – only in 2D - of course, Mrs Elliot would hand out any item such as today's memory cards to be used in the children's consoles. These would contain the tasks for the day and were often specifically programmed for each child.

The cards would have come directly from the Ministry of eEducation in the City each morning on the Net via secure download. They would have been prepared by the Ministry's AdminBots during the night and followed an appropriate sequence of lessons devised by the SyllabiiBots for each main subject. Naturally, all computing software and algorithms were supplied by the Cyber Ware company who had developed an international monopoly to match their universally-accepted system of Electrically Stimulated Learning (ESL).

Of course, not everything was done by computer at the Ministry of eEducation which had retained its archaic name from earlier times to give the public a sense of political stability. Each section of the grand educational plan (which was devised by Artificial Intelligence computers) for all grades from Intro to Exit had its own human 'Assistant Director of Education (Grade 2)' who was responsible for monitoring the grand educational plan for that section and to ensure that all of the appropriate downloads were made. This usually meant visually checking all of the specific consoles and ensuring that all of the many coloured lights flashed on at the appropriate time. These people were themselves supervised by the 'Assistant Director of Education' who watched her console which showed that her inferiors were monitoring their consoles. Occasionally, this worthy would report to the only other human in the ministry who was the actual Director of Education and answerable to no one else but his political master, the Minister of Education who usually was not available for comment, especially around election time.

Back at eSchool Primary #4069, each specific download of data would have been received by Mr Cribble, the eSchool's CompTech, who was responsible for all of the technical aspects of the eSchool. Each morning he would receive the downloads from the Ministry and then copy and paste all of the appropriate data to each class's master Memory Card which would then be placed into the appropriate eTech's box in the staff room. Each eTech would then have to check that this was appropriate for the day and then make multiple copies for each student. No overnight preparation was required by Mrs. Elliot nor any of the other eTechs; their function in the vast and intricate education system of the City was simply to care for the children, turn on the SurroundTV room screen and the individual consoles then handout the appropriate Memory Cards and software to the children. Occasionally the eTechs would have to assist with any problem that a child might have with the work or provide them with any physical help.

Of course, occasionally there would be the need for updates to the children's Electrically Stimulated

Learning (ESL) and Mrs. Elliot would then have to carefully attach each child's input socket to the main terminal modules at the back of the room. Here, each child had their own comfortable chair with their name artistically painted in colourful script. Emiliano's chair had his name painted in dark blue; his favourite colour. Each soft, comfortable chair also had head restraints so that the children could not move their necks once the download cables were plugged into the small, unobtrusive ports which were situated at the base of the back of their necks. Mrs. Elliot would carefully unlock the long cable locker which ran the entire length of the row of chairs and extend the cables out for each child. Next, she would then move along the row and insert each cable into the port of each child; usually with a gentle word:

"There you are, Emiliano! All done!"

Mrs Elliot was always very careful doing this. There could not be any doubt that each cable was firmly attached so that the update could be downloaded smoothly and completely. At first, the children found this procedure most unsettling, even with Mrs Elliot's calm and smiling explanation of the nature of the update and the need to remain perfectly still.

There would be a beautiful clip of quiet music and some peaceful scene – usually of a nice garden or cute animals – for the children to watch as a colourful hologram on the SurroundTV. This was both peaceful and ensured that the children would look in one direction and keep their necks still.

Updates usually only lasted no more than a few minutes and often occurred at the same time each month. They would contain data which would redefine, add to or generally improve the brain stimulations received at their 5+ Download. Today's update contained additional knowledge, skills and attitudes towards music and mathematics; two interconnected processes which would be further explored in next week's Memory Card tasks.

At the end of each update, Mrs. Elliot would quietly move along the row of chairs and unplug each child, usually with some soothing words such as:

"Well, now Emiliano! That wasn't too bad, was it?" She was usually right about the process as Emiliano would only feel a slight tickle at the back of his neck and a warm, fuzzy feeling in his head. His cable would be removed very gently and placed back into the long cable locker behind the row of chairs. When all of the children had been unplugged and their head restraints removed – but only then – Mrs Elliot would then always say:

"Ready! Don't move yet! There are plenty treats on the tables in the centre of the room so there will be no need to rush. There will be a special treat for the last one to get to the table." This last comment usually ensured that the children would get out of their comfortable chairs slowly and move with even greater stealth towards the small tables which she had placed near the blue thick-pile round floor mats. On each table would be many small plates with a variety of food and drink – mostly fruit, small round cheeses and crackers. Sometimes there would be olives, and small onions as well; Emiliano loved those treats the best. There were also many small, recyclable paper cups and jugs of fresh juices which Mrs Elliot would then pour out for each child. Update Day was no longer a source of apprehension but a party day. To Mrs Elliot, a compassionate person, this was the best part of an update and the only real time when the children socialised with each other without using an electronic device. Even during their two small recess times, which came precisely at 1100 and 1300 hours each day, the children would prefer to sit in silent little groups with their friends and use their phones to communicate to others more distant. This usually followed the usual line up for the bank of food and drink vending machines from the eBurger chain where they would use their food eCard to get what they wanted to eat and drink. Emiliano usually avoided the many different types of eBurgers and went for the fruit and desserts instead. Weird!

So after their update session, whilst the children ate and drank their treats and spoke together – usually too loudly for Mrs. Elliot's liking – she would close up the cable locker and make sure that the coded lock was reset. Neck cables were only licenced for educational institutions, some medical facilities and a few carefully vetted and licenced individuals such as General Neurosurgeons and eCounsellors. Possession of unlicensed cables was highly illegal and detection of their use out of prescribed hours or at unlicensed premises would quickly attract the attention of the police. It was commonly thought that Cyber Ware's own External Security Division was also monitoring such cable use or so it was suggested by some of the Conspiracy Journalists on the nightly eNews.

And so, the years passed at eSchool Primary #4069. Young Emiliano Montalban grew into a sturdy young lad; well, at least Grandfather Adam thought so. His mother thought otherwise. Young Emiliano was not like the rest of his eSchool mates and indeed any other children that she knew. Certainly, her many friends on Fritface agreed and commiserated with her and generally commented on eChat about poor Muriel Montalban's skinny son.

Grandfather Adam had spoken quietly to his grandson on one of the boy's many visits to his grandfather's ramshackled old house and had reassured him that he was not skinny at all. Rather, it was the rest of the world which was obese. That was a word which Grandfather Adam said quietly, almost in a whisper, was no longer used in polite speech. It was now considered to be derogatory and had once been a term of discrimination – just like the term skinny was now. Grandfather Adam gladly accepted that epithet when his grandson, like all children of his age displayed supreme honesty in their relationships with others and had pointed out that he too was not like the rest of the adult Montalban family. The old man had simply given a great sigh, smiled and stated the obvious that he was an old man and once one got over middle age of about sixty then one did not really care about one's appearance.

Emiliano had been thankful that his father, Stanley, had allowed him to visit his old grandfather when he got older. Grandfather Adam only lived a few blocks from Emiliano's home and as there was a visual tracking device on the boy's phone, there was no problem in seeing that he arrived safely. Emiliano's mother, Muriel was always worried about the boy's visits; but then again, she worried about most things.

"Watch out for the traffic!" she would instruct her son before he left. This was not really much of a concern in these modern times as traffic was always light, even at peak hour when most of the commuters travelled by autoBus to their factories and offices. The main traffic was well overhead as Hoverbot drones did much of the consignment of goods and mail.

"Don't talk to strangers!" she would say. Not that this would be a worry as people only went out on the streets to do specific things and did not waste their time to stop and talk to little boys. Ever since the great pandemics of the 2020s, most of the populations of the Greater Networked Cities spent most of the time at home except when going to a rare social event or to visit friends and relatives. Most items, especially eBurgers and other foods, were home delivered by the Hoverbots.

Emiliano liked visiting his grandfather because his old house held a lot of very interesting secrets, especially in all of the books which the old man kept in a large trunk upstairs in the attic. Emiliano would rummage through the trunk and find an interesting book, sometimes a novel written by some obscure twentieth century author, or sometimes a non-fiction on topics which were never downloaded at eSchool. Sometimes Emiliano would simply just sit with his grandfather in the dusty lounge room and listen to the stories of the old man's youth. Grandfather Adam had been a teacher; not an eTech shuffling Memory Cards and other items from child to child, but a real teacher who had to use his personality to impart real knowledge and skills to a classroom full of students. There were only a few eTablets then, but Grandfather Adam's classroom did have computers – PCs he called them – which could be used at certain times during the day. Mostly, he would tell the students interesting stories about his travels and of the geography of the countries which he had visited, because that was his teaching area, and he would supplement his whiteboard notes and their textbooks with paper maps, computer simulations and videos – only two dimensional, of course.

Emiliano did not know what a whiteboard was and he figured out that a textbook was a book that all of the students had from which they read of many marvellous things. Emiliano also liked reading; it enabled him to use his imagination instead of simply accepting the nature of the images and sounds on his eTablet or on the SurroundTV.

Sometimes Grandfather Adam would read him a story from one of his private collection. He especially liked the stories from an obscure author called Hernan Moreno Ruiz who lived back in the nineteenth century. He wrote about adventures in South America, a faraway continent where Grandfather Adam's great grandmother had come from. Emiliano would lie back in the old, dusty armchair and close his eyes and imagine the sounds, sights and smells of the rainforest and his hero cutting his way through the dense jungle looking for adventure or of the high, snow-capped mountains with a cold wind whistling past the llamas which quietly ate the grass of the high pastures.

Finally, Emiliano came to his final or exit year at eSchool Primary #4069 and sat for the Progression Exam which came down online directly from the Ministry of eEducation. It was what Grandfather Adam had called a Performance Test – partly testing their intelligence, knowledge of social content and how well they could perform various mental and skill tasks on screen. Based on this exam, students would be then be counselled as to the type of program in which they should enrol when they progressed onto eSchool Secondary in the following year. These Secondary programs were specifically aimed at either professions, trades or further studies later on at the online eUniversities.

Emiliano's final results from this test were very high in all aspects but his mother still had some concerns about his lack of social interaction; after all, he only had twenty friends on his Fritface account and his eTechs at eSchool Primary #4069 had often mentioned that he preferred individual rather than team eGames and simulations.

There were a great many potential Secondary programs which the young Emiliano could take. The choice of program would be made by the child's parents as the young child was not considered to have much of an opinion as to what he really wanted to be. This seemed to be a common and acceptable feature of societies of the Greater Networked Cities and even after they had progressed through Secondary and even eUniversity programs most students had little idea of where they were going. There were Secondary online programs which lead to careers in all manner of Trades, eCommerce, the Professions and, of course, in Computing. The Cyber Ware company was especially interested in the very brightest students, even offering valuable scholarships at the Secondary level for students to join their multinational monopoly. Emiliano Montalban was offered just such a scholarship but his father, Stanley, did not accept it for his son and Emiliano was thankful for that.

"Cryptocurrency is the way to go!" stated his father with much enthusiasm and determination.

His wife Muriel did not have many thoughts as to the final career of her little boy and so agreed with her husband to enrol their son into a 'Two Language eCommerce' program at the prestigious Saint Joseph of Cupertino eGrammar, Stanley's old Alma Mata. Poor Emiliano did not want to go into this program nor to this prestigious school, but he was not asked for his opinion.

So, on the first day of the school term in the next year, the autoBus coloured in the grammar school's colours of grey and black arrived outside of the Montalban' supersized residence at exactly 8:35 to take him to his new eSchool Secondary.

4.

Saint Joseph of Cupertino eGrammar was an old, well-established school, a part of the Superior Public Schools (SPS) of the City. Emiliano had a feeling of foreboding about this institution despite its great reputation. This was not helped by the video screen at the entrance to the autoBus which showed a stern-looking face of a non-smiling mature man with grey hair and glasses and a clerical collar which said in an equally stern-sounding monotone:

"Welcome to Saint Joseph of Cupertino eGrammar – you are one of us now!"

There was no fault here in the audio of the welcome. That would not have been tolerated at all at St. Cups as the school was commonly known.

Emiliano looked briefly at the stern, mature image with grey hair and glasses and thought of a passage he had read in one of Grandfather Adam's old books which had said:

'Abandon All Hope Ye Who Enter Here!'

So, he climbed up the steps and carefully moved up the aisle of the bus as its door shut tight and its soundless, electronic motors slowly brought the vehicle up to its sedate speed. A few heads of the other occupants, mostly children of a variety of ages all in their grey and black identical uniforms, were raised to look at the new arrival, but mostly they were engrossed in the games and messages on their phones or eTablets. There were also a few men sitting at the back of the bus looking rather stern in the humiliation that they should be in a school autoBus. They were human administrators who preferred to take the free bus than take their own cars off home charge.

The autoBus eventually drove through the impressive gateway of the school and up the long driveway to the even more impressive gothic-style building at its end. The building also seemed to be dressed in stone of the school colours of grey and black increasing Emiliano's apprehension even more.

The autoBus stopped at its final GPS node. The students slowly filed out. Most of the boys – for Saint Cups was only for boys – slowly walked off to their own Houserooms whilst Emiliano and a few others huddled together in a small group and looked around at their bleak surroundings. A cold wind blew across the open space in front of the grey and black building.

Eventually a mature, stern-looking man with grey hair, glasses and wearing a black academic gown and mortarboard came down the steps from the main double doorway of the school. Emiliano could not help but notice as one of the doors creaked open that it was made of a very heavy timber studded with iron. He wasn't sure whether the doors and the rest of fortress-like building was designed to keep the barbarians from beyond the Greater Networked Cities out or its unfortunate students in. This new grey man called himself Brother Tobias as he informed them that he was the school's Master of Studies.

"Follow me!" he said in a very low and stern voice and he walked back up the stairs and through the fortress' portal. Emiliano looked up as he walked through the door but did not see the teeth of a portcullis which he had expected hanging down. Brother Tobias led the group of frightened boys into a large hall, which he called the Great Hall. This had a ceiling of impressive archways in dark wood. All around the walls were long honour boards in lighter wood which listed the names of many past students and staff who had achieved some sort of fame at the school. Walking past one board which listed Masters who had been at the school for over thirty years, he noticed that the first such honour had been conferred in the year 1885. Reaching the front of the hall, Brother Tobias instructed all of the boys to sit.

"Fill up the first row first. No talking!" he said sternly as he mounted the steps to the stage which took up the entire width of the hall. Here he moved a lectern in dark wood and adjusted a small microphone which came out from its top. There was a row of folding chairs behind the lectern and after readjusting one, he then walked off to the side of the stage through the curtains.

Silence and the gothic look of the old hall did not help the students' personal comfort but no one dared utter a sound. Emiliano thought that he had entered one of Grandfather Adam's old novels and he would not have been surprised if he had seen a cloud of bats swooping down onto the unfortunates sitting in the second row; those who did not fill up the first row first.

Brother Tobias re-entered from Stage Left followed by a small group of men, similarly dressed in academic gowns and mortarboards, who moved across the stage and filled up the front row of the folding chairs first. Brother Tobias moved to the lectern:

"All stand!" he said in a loud and imposing voice and the men in the chairs behind quickly stood up. Emiliano and his fellows, including the bat-free boys in the second row, also stood up and looked around them.

An imposing man; tall but not as obese as Brother Tobias and the other Masters on the stage, walked in from Stage Left and placed a small pile of papers on the lectern. He also wore a long black academic gown and mortarboard but there was a wide fringe of white fur on a cape which was around his shoulder and he also had a black shirt with a white clerical collar.

"I am Father Isidore. I am the Headmaster of Saint Joseph of Cupertino eGrammar." He went on to give a rather neutral welcome to the school and a few details of how it had been established back in 1851 by an Order of the Church which no longer existed as it had failed to modernise at the end of the twentieth century and had widely denounced computers as the creation of the Devil. Since then, in more enlightened times, the school had been re-established by the new Brothers of the Progressive Order of Saint Helen (POSH) and had quickly embraced Electrically Stimulated Learning (ESL).

After the Headmaster's speech, which Emiliano thought would go on forever, he handed the microphone over to Brother Tobias who then read out a list of boys who would be in the various Grade 1 classes. As each list was read out for that class, a Master from the front row of seats would stand up to take the appointed group away to their new classrooms. Emiliano's name was read out on the list for the 'Two Language eCommerce' class which was to be taken by Brother Brian.

Brother Brian was not a mature man with grey hair and glasses but rather young, portly as expected, had red hair and a broad smile which seemed to be almost forbidden by the rest of the Masters. He led Emiliano's group of about fifteen other boys out of the Great Hall, across a bare stone quadrangle into another building of grey and black stone. Soon they stopped at a simple wooden door and Brother Brian asked them to line up along the windowed wall in two lines, filling up from the left first.

"Dis is ooehr classroom." He said in a broad Irish accent. "Go in un set in de chairs boeht be sure and fell oehp de first row first o' all"

Not sure of exactly what Brother Brian had said, the boys entered the room, left hand line followed by the right and then sat down in the chairs, filling up the first row first. That seemed to be the safest way of things here. Emiliano was not sure as to what two languages Brother Brian would teach. English should at least be one of them.

As it eventuated, Brother Brian actually taught eGeography much to Emiliano's delight because this, thanks to Grandfather Adam, was his favourite subject. English was to be taught by Brother Jerome, History was to be taught by Brother Francis, eCommerce by Brother Matthew, Mathematics by Brother Herbert and Spanish by Brother Santiago. Mandarin was to be their other language, but as yet no eTech could be found to manage that subject. Those aspirants who were very fluent in this language had found more lucrative employment elsewhere as staff in Chinese online take-aways. As with the rest of the education systems within the Greater Networked Cities, all of these subjects were really eSubjects that were taught online using the same downloads and updates sent out to the state-owned schools using software supplied by Cyber Ware. This fact was not overtly announced by St Cups, as they had a traditional school culture to maintain and it suited the staff, most of whom were eTechs like all of the others in eSchools, to think of themselves in the old style as Masters.

In many respects, Emiliano got to like the daily atmosphere of St. Cups. Regardless of its widely announced traditional school culture of excellence in everything and the arrogance of its school motto *"Melius in Omnibus[1]"* which said as much. Emiliano found many of the Masters – eTechs – actually quite friendly and open in their classroom styles. It was only when the Headmaster appeared that silence and obedience reared their ugly heads. Brother Brian, especially loved to talk – if one could understand his broad Irish accent – about the many countries he had visited. His geography lessons included classification of towns and cities by the number of pubs, especially Irish Pubs, that they fostered.

---

[1] "Better at Everything"

"Now Bresbane, Aoehstralia 'as t'ree good Iresh poehbs. An' so tis! An' so tis!" he would say.

Emiliano and his classmates soon got to know the difference between 'To be sure, to be sure' (probably an exaggeration) and 'An' so it is, An' so it is' (the truth). Despite his brogue, Brother Brian was an excellent eTech and his students loved going to his classes. Not only did he anticipate any problems which they may have, he regularly illustrated some of the boring online geography lessons with some of his personal stories and artefacts that he had gathered when back-packing around the world. Emiliano especially liked his stories about South America:

"Now! Ded I tell you abooeht me trep down de Amazahn where I was adahpted by sahme Spider Mahnkeys?" Brother Brian would say much to the students' delight, many imagining Brother Brian sitting up in the trees talking in his Irish accent to the monkeys - an' so it is, an' so it is.

Emiliano soon discovered that St Cups still had many vestiges of a traditional grammar school regardless of its pretence to be a progressive eSchool. Grandfather Adam would clap his hands and grin when Emiliano recounted some of the strange practices which often went on within the classroom when the Headmaster or other senior staff were not around. There was even a very dusty room filled with books – not an eLibrary like the one which could download pdfs online – but a real one with real books. Brother Anthony was in charge of the school's eLibrary, a small gothic building in black and grey stone slightly separated from the other buildings. Emiliano thought that Brother Anthony was also as ancient as the school's buildings and one day, when he went into the eLibrary to get a download of a recent book called '200 Years Before the Mast', he had discovered a small, unobtrusive door in the far corner of the room which Brother Anthony had left open. The old Brother had gone into what was part of the old library to look up an ancient manuscript about the old Windows 15 Operating System. Emiliano, curious as ever, had followed the old Brother into the large, dusty room which had cobwebs handing from its arched ceiling and had marvelled at the many shelves of equally dusty old books.

"Whadya doin' 'ere?" snorted the old brother angrily when he had turned around and found the young boy standing open-mouthed in the doorway.

Brother Anthony was indeed old and had been given the simple job of eLibrarian to keep the dust off the computers in his final years when even the task of being an eTech was considered too much for the old man. Besides, his rough upbringing on the docks of the City and his crude way of speaking was not appreciated by some of the boys whose parents expected a higher level of language in an eGrammar school.

"Nothing, sir," Emiliano had stuttered. "I was just looking at all of those lovely books."

There was just the hint of a cynical smile on Brother Anthony's face:

"Wadya know abart books. Boy? He said in his usual gravelly voice.

"I read them sometimes in my grandfather's library, but he only has a few books. You must have hundreds here! That is truly wonderful" he said, a genuine look of amazement on his young face.

The old librarian came over and put his equally old hand onto the boy's shoulder and smiled.

"It's rare ta' I hear any of the young'uns 'ere talk about real books an' not jest abarht them electrical eThingies they download. Yer can't feel the pages and smell tha' paper with them things. Come in an' 'av a good look." He said with a sweep of his arm.

Emiliano went in to the room which he found was quite large with old tiles on the floor and a high arched ceiling. Dust and cobwebs covered everything, but there were rows and rows of books extending off in the gloom.

"I don' get much time ta do cleanin' mind. But all of these prec'us volumes are catalogued according to Dewey." The old librarian said apologetically but with just a hint of pride.

Emiliano slowly walked down one of the aisles and looked at the many books – mostly with identical bindings all covered in dust. 'What treasure!' he thought. He pulled one book from the shelf and found that it had been printed way back in 1976. It was a book entitled 'Modern Technology' and as he thumbed through the pages it reminded him of one of Brother Francis' history lessons. There were sections on how petroleum was taken out of the ground and actually used as a fuel and another section on how computers would one day have memories of up to one megabyte.

Emiliano would often visit Brother Anthony who would quietly lend him one of the dusty books from his secret library. The boy would hide it in the folds of his grey and black blazer and carry it to Grandfather Adam's house where the two of them would delight in the printed pages and what they contained. Grandfather Adam would often request a certain topic and back at the school, Brother Anthony would happily find such a book for the other old man who appreciated the printed page.

Emiliano's life at the school throughout his five years there were generally happy. He loved some of the stories from Brother Brian who continued as Emiliano's eTech (geography) for several years and also, he had found that whilst most of the other Masters still had the same traditional and personal views about eTech-student interaction, some would occasionally vary their interpretation of some of the downloads and add some physical item or simulation to make their subject more personal and interesting.

Physical eEducation was a problem for the growing Emiliano. He generally liked sport but there was little real physical activity involved and his fellow students did little which would change their normal rotund shapes. Emiliano was not considered to be what the Master of eSport, Brother Sebastian, would call a 'team player'. On Wednesday afternoons, which was entirely devoted to eSport, Emiliano would enter the huge metal eSports Hall which was constructed way out near what had once been the old school's sporting fields. It was almost as though the shiny, austere structure had been cast out by the rest of the eGrammar's black and grey buildings. Emiliano would wander over to the Sports Hall with the rest of the school after the deep tolling of the eGrammar's bells signalled the end of their second recess. Inside, the students would go to their preferred consoles to begin their 'sports period'. He would find a console which had an individual eGame, preferably one which required some sort of physical body movement in response to the instructions or cues which appeared on the screen. Failing to find an appropriate console available, he would go over to one of the corners, well away from the others, and do some personal body exercises which he had found in one of Brother Anthony's old books on 'Isotonic Exercises'. Naturally the other students thought that such actions without a console or WIFI handset was totally unnatural and would laugh at Emiliano and make unkind comments about his skinny body shape and weird behaviour. These hurtful comments came mostly from the jocks who were on the school's eFootball team and played their frantic matches against other eGrammar schools wired up in front of the big wall-size SurroundTV screen at the far end of the hall.

Emiliano put these jibes aside and got on with his life. Like most young boys he would have preferred to be as popular as those who achieved fame at eSports, but as he was successful at his academic subjects he did not mind. He had also quietly changed his subject choices over the years so that eCommerce had silently been confined to the boring gloom of finance and he had taken up eScience instead. At least he found that more interesting even if old Brother Albert appeared to be mentally addled at times and would often get confused about the nature of a chemical reaction when some students dropped red ink into their beaker.

At the end of the year, Emiliano had sat in the draughty Grand Hall and had completed his Final Exit Exam online at his console and had achieved excellent scores in all of his subjects. Father Isidore, the Headmaster had been pleased with Emiliano's exam results and was prepared to recommend him to a prestigious eUniversity but Emiliano chose, without his parent's blessing, to enrol in the local eTech college instead. When it was too late to rescind this decision, Emiliano had broken the news to his stunned parents. His father, Stanley was very disappointed that his son would not be a cryptocurrency trader like himself and his mother, Muriel simply wept at the thought of her brilliant son becoming a mere eTech. What would her many friends on Fritface and eChat on her Superior A-Network say? But Emiliano Montalban left St. Cups a happy young man and looked forward to his own, independent future. He did not feel any urge to make such any comment on his Fritface account.

5.

Emiliano's first year out of school was a momentous one for several reasons. Firstly, he had secured a scholarship to go to the Andersen College of eTechnology – a subsidiary of the mighty Cyber Ware company and the main training institution for eTechs in the City. It was a whole three months course during which he would receive all of the downloads required for his new occupation. There would be downloaded packages in the use of all of the Cyber Ware programs which were used in Electrically Stimulated Learning (ESL); the use of simulations and eGames to reinforce the learning from these packages; skills in using the Upload terminal modules and equipment; the care and maintenance of student Insert connections; and even a short course on Child ePsychology and simple basic maintenance of an eSchool classroom.

The downloads were very easy to accept as Emiliano had been retested by the College's General Neurosurgeon and found to have exceptional memory capacity and synapse speed for download transmission. There were updates every week as new products from Cyber Ware came online; in fact, there was a rumour going around the College that the company was going to go public and make many of its new programs available to all those who could afford them without the need to go to an eSchool or eUniversity.

Emiliano finished his three months training with only the minimum of daily headaches and then started his three months as an Assistant eTech. After that, he could be employed as an eTech in any eSchool Primary but would have to go through a probationary period of six months to obtain the approval of his Master eTech before he would finally achieve his Certificate of eTechnology. In this post-training period, Emiliano was very fortunate as he was able to obtain his Assistant's position at his old eSchool Primary #4069 where Mrs. Gabriella Elliot was now the Principal.

After his many years away from his old eSchool Primary, he found that Mrs Elliot was a little further past what one might call her youth, even becoming mature and her hair was now grey, well most of it, but it was still tied behind with a bright pink ribbon and she now wore glasses. She still smiled a lot and still neatly dressed in some bright colour and Emiliano thought that she was still the most wonderful person he had ever met.

He wondered however what he might look like after a few years in the job; mature of age, grey hair and glasses perhaps? He shuddered at that thought and every morning before going to work, he would look at his sleek black hair in the mirror of his tiny room in the Montalban supersized residence and check for any signs of grey. After all, he was almost nineteen years of age.

He learnt a lot from Mrs Elliot who ran her eSchool Primary with the utmost care and happiness. His Master eTech, Mr. Norman, was also a rare character as most eTechs in eSchool Primary were women. There was nothing strange about Mr Norman's behaviour, despite some of the insinuations made by a few of the parents who seemed to be more rotund than most and obviously listened to the wrong eFriends on Fritface. Mr Norman was an enthusiastic eTech who made his students laugh with silly little jokes as he handed out equipment or helped them with their online work. When it came to the weekly update, he would attach each student to the main terminal module at the back of the room with some amusing flourish:

"Zap! – all plugged in" or "1, 2, 3 – plugged" or for children who were obsessed with eGames such as

Brutal Combat he would say "Locked and loaded, soldier!"

Sometimes, Mr Norman would go beyond his eTech brief and give some special care to any child who was finding some of the content of the daily Memory Card program difficult. Mr Norman had had great experience outside of the eSchool; he had been a soldier in the war in Africa specialising in electronic counter surveillance and had then worked for the United Nations there after the war. He knew what it was like for the children of poor countries who were not connected to the International Net and did not therefore have the benefits of Electrically Stimulated Learning (ESL). He had helped some of the local people run their little mud-brick and thatch schools and had enjoyed the interaction with the children who asked for very little and usually received much less. He marvelled at how some of the locals had imparted sufficient knowledge and skills so that their children could become useful individuals when they grew up – if they got that far! Emiliano finished his initial Assistant eTech period and at eSchool Primary #4069 and came away a much better person, thanks to Mrs Elliot again and of course, Mr Norman.

He was also lucky to secure his Probationary eTech period at his other old school, Saint Joseph of Cupertino eGrammar, although his father, Stanley, suggested that it had more to do with his 'Old Boys' contacts than mere luck. It did not matter that he was ePrimary trained, as St Cups was always short of eTechs and not being a member of its religious Order was also unimportant as long as he accepted the lower salary. He was pleased to find that his old eTech, Brother Brian was now the Master of Studies at the school and that Brother Anthony, much older and certainly dustier, was still the ancient librarian.

"Now den. Welcomb back me bahy. It's good to see ya an' so it tis, an' so it tis. Ya can 'ave one o' de junior grades in eGeography and i'll 'elp you dere to be sure an all," said Brother Brien with a smile when Emiliano first reported to the institution on his first day. Emiliano was very happy to be back. This was especially true now that the austere Father Isidore had left to become the City's new eBishop and had been replaced by a more genial character, Father Vincent, a mature grey-haired man with glasses who spent most of his time in his office and always smelt of whiskey.

The second major event of his first year out of school was the tragic death of his parents, Stanley and Muriel. They had been sitting out in the garden of their supersized residence when a Hoverbot drone, carrying a large consignment of food materials from the City warehouse to the local eBurger chain suffered a power loss which caused it to go off course and crash into the Montalban's summerhouse, killing its two occupants.

Emiliano was momentarily distraught at the loss of his parents and quite a few of his parent's Fritface friends added insincere comments of sympathy to his own Fritface account. Many of the people who lived in the same street but who had had no personal contact with the Montalban Family, piled bouquets of flowers up against the front fence where they went rotten after a few days and Emiliano had to call in a special garbage collection to remove the stinking heap.

Stanley Montalban, who had made his fortune in cryptocurrency trading, left this substantial amount entirely to Emiliano, minus a healthy bequest to St. Cups. Now Emiliano was finally able to achieve his long-term ambition of opening his own eSchool Primary.

At the end of his year at St. Cups, he once again said goodbye to Brothers Brian and Anthony and waved farewell to Father Vincent who had been looking uncomprehendingly out of his window and walked down the long road towards the front gate of St. Cups.

The cryptocurrency which his father had left him enabled him to purchase an eSchool licence and download licenced programs and Memory Cards from the Ministry of eEducation, which also acted as the official agency of Cyber Ware. His new eSchool Primary was located in the large front room of the Montalban supersized residence. Emiliano had hired a casual CompTech to install all of the official and licenced connections to the main terminal module and all of the many individual models for the many students which he expected to enrol in the new year. Five students and their parents arrived on the first day of the eSchool in response to Emiliano's advertisements on his Fritface page and on his new, online corporate Netpage.

Not a great start, Emiliano thought, but then again, it was a start after all, even if most of the parents had been local eFriends of his parents and who had been able to secure the appropriate autoBus connections from their equally supersized residences.

Emiliano was determined to make his eSchool the best in the City and he was also determined to add his own personal touches which he had learnt from Mrs Elliot, Brother Brian and Mr. Norman. He also had visited Grandfather Adam who had given him some old fashioned but good practical advice about his days before the introduction of Electrically Stimulated Learning (ESL) and its eTechs. Grandfather Adam had also given his grandson some real books on a subject called 'Teaching' as well as others of great interest, even if the technology described had become obsolescent. Brother Anthony also sent over a collection of books by the eGrammar's own blue and black Hoverbot drone so that Emiliano was able to establish a small library of real books in the Breakfast Room of his supersized residence. He would use these books and many of the stories from the life of Brother Brian and Mr. Norman to supplement the downloads, upgrades, eGames and simulations which officially came from the Ministry and Cyber Ware.

The next event of great significance to Emiliano's future was the change in the corporate direction of

Cyber Ware. The earlier rumour had been true. Having long secured an international monopoly in licenced computer software and packages for Electrically Stimulated Learning (ESL) in all state-run and private eSchools, Cyber Ware now went public and offered new and exciting downloads directly to individuals who could afford them.

Now most individuals in all of the Greater Networked Cities (GNC) across the globe in what was still archaically called the 'Free world' had been educated by direct download via their brain implants. Erez Anderson, the enigmatic head of Cyber Ware had long dreamed of tapping into the personal and DIY needs of this extensive market. Even the greatly populated countries of China and Russia were potential markets for the new downloads, even if there had been extensive 'Software Piracy' going on in these countries for years. Both the Russian Democratic Federation and the Unified Chinese People's Popular Democracy had long ago maintained that their own home-grown systems of Electrically Stimulated Learning (ESL) had been developed in their own countries even if many of the packages bore a startling resemblance to the originals from Cyber Ware. This was of little concern to Erez Andersen as he had his own Espionage and Acquisition Division which also had produced authentic packages in Russian and Mandarin. Furthermore, he had correctly reasoned that many of the elite in both countries, and certainly those wealthy individuals in the poorer countries in Eastern Europe, Africa and South America who had been educated by direct download, would jump at the chance to be seen as having the latest and internationally acceptable Cyber Ware packages.

Initially to some eTechs, these packages seemed to be a threat to those downloaded in eSchools, but Emiliano saw them as simply another dimension of adult eEducation. So far, most of the available packages were of the simple hobby and DIY type with a few exotic eTravel virtual holidays.

Soon however, the big news which was heralded on both eChat, Fritface and all of the SurroundTV channels was all about a new Cyber Ware personal download called the 'Socially Acceptable Package (SAP)'. This package claimed, according to all of the beautiful young people and media personalities seen on the advertisements, would give those privileged people who downloaded the package, great popularity and access to a vast range of eFriends. It was the 'must have' for all of those people who felt that they should mean something in eSociety and could make a major impact in the future. If one wanted to succeed in life then THIS was the package for you!

The downside of this download was that the licence for this package was very expensive and therefore well beyond the reach of everyone except the elite of society. But then again, this was the market target which Erez Andersen at Cyber Ware had envisaged for his new download and so a date and time was widely advertised for the first release of the SAP download. Willing buyers frantically paid their cryptocurrency via PayMate and received their hardware by Cyber Ware's own Hoverbot drones which would enable them to connect their new licenced cables between their neck sockets and their personal computers. Many unfortunates who were too slow to respond to the mass advertising campaign and missed the payment deadline by only a few minutes loudly complained on Fritface and eChat.

Emiliano had never seen himself as one of the City's elites and he also had plans for the rest of his late father's fortune to be put into improvements for his little eSchool. When the day and the time came for the worldwide download of the Socially Acceptable Package, Emiliano was busy perusing his small library to find interesting stories which he could tell his students. He particularly liked the one from his favourite author, Hernan Moreno Ruiz called '*The Little Lost Alpaca*'.

The day after the great world download of the SAP, Emiliano called all of his students to the centre of the room where they would comfortably lay down on the cushions on the soft pile blue mats and closed their eyes whilst he read them this story. It was about a little boy called Carlos who lived in the high mountains of Peru and who had a pet Alpaca which he had called 'Sumaq' which meant 'beautiful one' in the local Quechua language. Emiliano had described the long snowy white fur of Sumaq and the high mountains of snow which surrounded the narrow Altiplano or high plains of Peru. He even described the sweet smells of the wildflowers which grew in the high plains. Naturally, he had not personally experienced such things, but Grandfather Adam's books did contain many such descriptions. He also found many imaginative descriptions in the novel and also in many picture books from Brother Anthony's library. The students were asked to imagine the surroundings of the

Peruvian Altiplano: the gentle but cold breezes blowing off the snow-capped mountains, the fragrances of the alpine grasses and flowers which also grew there and the faces and colourful dress of Carlos and his father, 'Papa Alberto'.

Emiliano went on with the story and told how Papa Alberto and Carlos were taking their llamas – bigger versions of the camel-like alpaca – to the high summer pastures. But one night, whilst high in the mountains, the naughty Sumaq had broken away and had run off to join the wild and free vicuñas who were the undomesticated version of the llama. The children giggled when Emiliano imitated the calls of the wild vicuñas who were calling little Sumaq to join them:

"Squeeku, squeeku, squeeku" Emiliano called in a high-pitched voice, imitating the sounds of the wild vicuñas.

The children grasped the edges of their thick piled blue mats and curled it around their bodies when Emiliano described how Carlos had also run off in the cold night to find his little lost Sumaq. Carlos finally found his Sumaq and the two were forced to snuggle up under a large rock for the night. The children shook when Emiliano described the bitter cold air of the night and the wind whistling down off the high, snow-capped and foreboding mounts where the Apus or gods of the mountains lived. Finally, the children uttered squeals of delight when Emiliano described how the next morning, Inti the sun finally came to the cold valley and how the little alpaca Sumaq, led his boy Carlos back down the mountain where they met Papa Alberto coming up the trail to find them.

Emiliano found that he enjoyed his personal interaction with his students and they enjoyed his stories and some of the interesting objects and books which was able to show them. Two of the parents objected to this, insisting that eTechs should simply serve the children's needs whilst they learnt online but others also enrolled their children in Emiliano's little school because they had heard via eChat and Fritface that his methods gave the children much happiness and an extra personal dimension in their early development. Emiliano did not know at that time that his personal approach was to receive considerable attention in the future.

6.

The major event which had a great effect on Emiliano's future came just after the much-anticipated release day of Cyber Ware's Socially Acceptable Package (SAP). It was extremely popular amongst the elite and privileged around the world, especially by the trendy young adults who saw it as a 'must have' so that they could put up the word of their new purchase to their friends on Fritface. A few of the world's leaders also saw it as a way of improving their popularity amongst the voters, especially if their form of government did not have the people's confidence. In the Kremlin, Premier Ivan Rasputin and in Beijing, General Secretary Gāo Yī both directly downloaded the new package claiming that this was for the benefit of their country and naturally claiming that their packages were really developed first in their own countries.

It was soon noticed locally, and then heralded internationally by the world's ePress that strange things were happening to many of the young adults and some of the older members of the world's elite who had downloaded the SAP package. They all seemed to exhibit complete disinterest in their family life, in their studies and their occupations and indeed in anything else requiring some detailed thought and responsibility, especially in world affairs. They tended to spend most of their time on their phones using eChat and Fritface, or the local home-grown equivalents, babbling on about trivial events and inane things which they were doing each day.

Some in-depth investigative journalism by one of the more hard-nosed American SurroundTV channels discovered, more by informed accident than skill, that the strange behaviour of those who had downloaded the SAP was due to a computer virus which had been inserted deep within the package. Further investigations involving the bribing and blackmailing of some of the employees of Cyber Ware's headquarters revealed that this virus had been inserted by the chief programmer who had actually developed the program. He had been sacked (without benefits) personally by the Chairman, Erez Andersen, only a few days before the final development and release of the package. The truth soon came out that this programmer had been greatly offended because his name was not going to be included on in the credits of the package – which only named Erez Andersen as the chief developer. As a consequence of this insult, the programmer had quickly inserted an additional sub-routine into the master program which was then mass produced and released with disastrous effects on all those who had downloaded it.

The world was aghast at what had happened. Many countries called upon their leaders who were still mentally competent to appeal to the United Nations to do something through their UNESCO sub-committee. At an extraordinary meeting of the UN Headquarters in Nairobi, which had been relocated from New York following disagreements with the United States about finance, most of the member states had voted to censure Cyber Ware and to look at the whole issue of Electrically Stimulated Learning (ESL). Naturally, without exception, the members who had voted to adopt this resolution came from the poorer countries which had not had much access to ESL and had resented the dominance of those countries who did have it and of the arrogance of some of their elite who had risen to wealth and power by being educated by it. The usual veto from the most powerful nations at the UN, namely the United States, Russia, China, the United Kingdom and France did not come about as expected because their leaders had either been downloaded with official or home-grown versions of SAP or influenced by others behind the scenes who had.

In the Kremlin, Premier Ivan Rasputin and in Beijing, General Secretary Gāo Yī sat stunned at their desks watching pop culture on SurroundTV or babbling incoherently to their mystified friends on eChat about the programs that they were watching. The Americans had abstained as President Quibbly already had too much to cope with a plethora of important bills being opposed by a hostile Senate and having to put down a resurrection of the 'Good Ole Boys' in the South with excessive firepower from the National Guard following his attempt to revoke the Second Amendment. The United Kingdom and France were too occupied with their economic and cultural battle in Britain's attempt to re-join the European Economic Community.

And so, all around the countries of the Greater Networked Cities (GNC), where their most influential people and leaders had reverted to the social responsibilities typical of the 15+ download, eSchools and eUniversities suddenly lost students as people feared that this new ePandemic would spread to all packages being downloaded and refused to allow themselves or their children to receive any more direct downloads or updates from Cyber Ware. Fritface and eChat were full of improbable 'fake news' about how this computer virus was spreading and how one could prevent it from infecting the downloaded. Investigative Journalists on several of SurroundTV's more sensational channels spread conspiracy theories far and wide.

As the Cyber Ware company had the world monopoly in Electrically Stimulated Learning (ESL), its shares fell through the floor in all of the stock markets around the world. There was some retention of ESL in counties which had pirated Cyber Ware products but soon they too began to experience popular uprisings of young adults and parents. The eMedia nightly showed mass demonstrations around the world with people marching in the streets with the burning of several eSchools and physical violence to eTechs in general. Computers, and indeed many other electrical devices such as SurroundTV consoles, microwaves and blenders often were to be seen in smashed piles on street corners.

Naturally there also nightly interviews with various people who suddenly claimed expertise in such matters, stating that they knew that this would happen despite having had the benefits of ESL themselves but being too poor to have downloaded the SAP. The International Union of eTechs also protested loud and long about the threats and mass unemployment of its members.

In his own little eSchool, Emiliano was unimpressed by all of the eMedia fuss and felt that perhaps the demise of Cyber Ware and ESL was a good thing and could possibly usher in a new era of real and socially rewarding learning.

When he had started his little eSchool, Emiliano had taken the precaution of saving some of the better packages of knowledge and skills from each of the main 5+, 12+ and 15+ then TERTed downloads – all illegally of course - thanks to the hacking skills of one of his few personal friends. He had also saved the best of the updates, eGames and simulations from Cyber Ware and had found that some of Grandfather Adam's old stand-alone programs from the earlier twenty-first century were still very useful and could be emulated on his own computers.

Emiliano now took a bold step and readvertised his little school – not as his eSchool, but a real school –

as an offline institution where students of all ages could receive an education without the threat of implanted viruses and control by the Cyber Ware company. Students were to be taught by real teachers, not maintenance-only eTechs in a socially interactive environment of happy face-to-face learning.

Emiliano had then disconnected all of the direct download apparatus and sent back his licenced cables and other paraphernalia to the now disorganised Ministry of eEducation and to the failed Cyber Ware company. He however, retained his parent's old Superior A-Network and the cable functions of his SurroundTV. With a little bit of electronic tinkering by his hacker friend, Emiliano was able to connect his saved simulations, eGames and some of the best educational programs to the SurroundTV monitor to be used as an offline display.

There suddenly was a very high local demand for enrolments at his little school which went well beyond the front rooms of his supersized residence. He firstly hired some of the trusted and more socially adventurous eTechs who he had met during his initial training and then taught them, on the job mainly, how to teach using their own skills and personalities along with his saved Memory Cards and downloaded eGames and simulations.

Mrs. Elliot from his old eSchool Primary #4069 and some of the other Principals from nearby eSchools came to him for advice now that their own institutions had become devoid of students and were receiving no support nor common sense from the Ministry as the Minister and Assistant Minister had also downloaded the SAP virus.

Even Brother Brian from St. Cups showed up one day claiming that:

"Now to be shoore! Tis a foine day fahr a renooal o' de ahld ways o' education" and asked if Emiliano could come back to the rebranded Saint Joseph of Cupertino Grammar School.

Other former eSchools and eGrammars also heard of Emiliano's new method of instruction – now touted by the popular press (without the 'e') as the Montalban Method – also wanted his services to train their old eTechs as teachers. The union was onside with all of this new use of its members so too was the City's new Ministry of eEducation, although reluctantly as they had to wait for their political masters to accept the new ideas, especially those who had not yet gone past their 15+ mentality. Other Ministries of the rest of the Greater Networked Cities also had these problems as well as finding out how to administer this new style of imparting knowledge, skills and appropriate attitudes without the use of mass downloads.

As AdminBots and SyllabiiBots could no longer be trusted with development of curriculum and education using Artificial Intelligence, many well-educated people were taken on to administer and develop new curricula. There was some objection from the now militant International Union which had deleted the term eTech from their name and added Teachers instead. They claimed that specific group educational expertise was needed for each subject area and age level in the Ministry to write the new curricula, although some ancient cynics such as Grandfather Adam, had commented such expertise had never been noted in the senior staff of the Ministry, even before the advent of the AdminBots.

Emiliano found to his surprise that he was now in great demand as a trainer of the new class of teachers rather than just being one himself. Having quickly and only partially trained his own staff and that of St Cups and some of the former local eSchools, he was now invited to the local University (now without the 'e') to help set up a teacher training program in their new Faculty of Education. This was going to be a challenge. Luckily, Grandfather Adam still had all of his old textbooks on teaching and their copyright, thankfully, now had expired. With these books and some other old training manuals, especially the no-nonsense pamphlets from Grandfather Adam's old military training, Emiliano was able to rewrite a comprehensive set of lecture materials for the new intake of teacher trainees at the university.

Firstly, he had to retrain many of the former eTechs who had worked at the university and who insisted that, despite many personality defects, that they did not need any more training. Some of the other academic Heads of Faculty showed some reactionary inclinations towards this new Education Faculty, but they were soon quietened when the Vice Chancellor threatened to end their tenure unless they were also trained in the Montalban Method.

So, it came as a new world order, that the Montalban Method spread across the world into all of the

Greater networked Cities and beyond. Many of the poorer nations, who had not had the advantage of ESL, continued with their previously derided methods of teaching in their poor, mud brick schools. It was not uncommon for a teacher in such a school to give an enigmatic knowing smile and a shake of their head when missionaries came to their country offering to set them up with the new Montalban Method.

For his part, Emiliano now realised that all of his hard work over the many years talking about and training people in his new non-electronically downloaded method, had brought about a personal change. He continued to be happy about his own career and that the world had become a better place where teachers and students now had real satisfaction within the classroom. But he had also found one day, when looking at the blurred image in his mirror at his home in the old supersized residence, that he was now becoming a mature-age man with most of his hair turning grey and that he would soon need classes. So he retired from teaching and the world of education and found a new joy in writing and publishing books – not eBooks, although they still had a place in the world – but real books made from paper where the readers could use their newly found non-electronic imaginations to travel to new places and have new adventures in their non-electronic minds.

STEELWIND

1.

Ship's Log of the Cetacean II: *0800 hours Sunday, 17th December, 2045. Position 37.53S, 178.76W; Winds moderate from the NW at 15 knots and abating. Heading 157 degrees; Sky clear. A new adventure begins….*

We had sat in the tiny cabin of John's little yacht as we watched him put the first entry into his new logbook with an exaggerated flourish of his pencil. He was a romantic in character, and strongly disapproved of the modern voicelogs, which had been introduced to commercial shipping some years ago. These had now become popular with amateur yachtsmen. He thought that they were too much like the so-called social media of his youth on which shallow-minded individuals communicated their personal trivia to their equally shallow multitude of 'friends'.

Now we were about 15 days out of Auckland enjoying the start of a new day. Our little yacht, the *Cetacean II,* a neat Sun Seeker 12 metre had performed beautifully across the Southern Pacific; a place notorious for its sudden storms. We were running before the wind, doing about eight knots. The little boat was only heeling a little, so the three of us sat comfortably on the inside of the Port gun'le[1]. Nobby had the wheel. He was doing a good job as helmsman despite his lack of sailing experience. We had shortened sail the previous night when the wind conditions were stronger, so John, the owner and skipper of the yacht reached over and let out the mainsail winch a few more notches. Mono and I were content just to add some ballast by sitting on the gun'le, our legs hanging over the side, our arms wrapped around the safety rail as we drank our early morning coffee which Mono had brought up from the yacht's small galley.

We were a mixed bunch on board the compact *Cetacean II* which was a stable little craft. John had learned his yachting skills close inshore on his previous yacht, a smaller Hood 20, which he had named *Cetacean* after the little outline of a breaching happy whale on its forward hull. John Foster was a Marine Insurance Underwriter in the city of Auckland. He had been born and raised on Herne Bay Beach in that city, just a short distance from the large marina of the Royal New Zealand Yacht Squadron. He naturally had a love for the sea as he had been a Junior in the club and then a full member since he was old enough to sail. Luckily, his father

---

[1] gun'le – or gunwale, the side edge of a boat or ship.

had been a Commodore of the club and was well off, so the young Foster was able to take sailing lessons at an early age. He had taken up sailing in OK Dinghies mostly, before crewing on several of the Squadron's yachts until he had enough money to purchase the first *Cetacean*. This current cruise, in his new yacht *Cetacean II*, was his most ambitious voyage so far and Skipper, as he liked to be called, had planned to take us all to the Chatham Islands some thousand kilometres south east from Auckland. As I had said before, he was a romantic of sorts, and probably imagined himself as an 'ancient mariner' right down to his full beard and the smelly old pipe which was rarely out of his mouth.

Knobby was the new hand on the wheel. His real name was Cornell Walsh, a 20-year-old apprentice carpenter from Auckland, but in true naval tradition, he had been nicknamed 'Nobby' as the skipper thought that 'Cornell' was rather pretensions for some obscure reason. The skipper had known Nobby since they had first met when the young teen had joined the Junior Sail Training Scheme and sailed small skiffs at the RNZYS, but this was the first time that the young man had ventured out to sea. Nobby was one of those skinny, red-headed, enthusiastic types who always had a smile on his freckled face and was willing to try anything. People of his age always thought of themselves as indestructible.

Mono also had high spirits, nothing much seemed to get him down. He also was a native of Auckland, about the same age as the skipper. As a Marine Surveyor in the city, he had met the Skipper through one of their many corporate connections soon becoming good friends. The skipper called him 'Mono' because his real name was Monir Khoury and he always seemed to be single minded in his views, especially about sailing. Nobby, who did not have the widest view of the world as well, once remarked that Mono reminded him of the character Corporal Klinger in the old classic TV show M.A.S.H. with his irrepressible nature and Middle Eastern facial features. Mono was in fact, a third generation Lebanese New Zealander who took Nobby's good-natured appellation with equally good humour. He was probably more 'New Zealandish' than the rest of the crew.

For my part, I was the 'odd-man out' in the crew, having hailed from Sydney Australia, where I worked as an Electrical Engineer who had done some sailing around Sydney Harbour. I was a little younger than Skipper. This was also my first voyage in a small yacht; most of my work at sea had been on the new generation of motor vessels which required my services whilst in port. I was more at home in the engine room of a cargo ship appraising the design and efficiency of the new marine electric motors and their batteries or their solar arrays on deck. With my name being Scott Campbell, I was naturally called 'Scotty' by the rest of the crew and most of my other friends for that matter. I had met the Skipper at a Marine Expo in Sydney back in 2030 and taken him out on the harbour in a small yacht belonging to a friend from the Vaucluse Yacht Club. We had kept in touch since then, and, as my annual leave had come up at the same time as Skipper's new voyage, I had been invited along as crew.

Our little yacht was called a Sun Seeker 12, she was little over twelve metres in length with a wide beam. She seemed to be a good sailor in a variety of winds but so far, we had been lucky enough to avoid the storms which often occurred in this part of the Pacific at this time of year. I had had some trepidation about venturing far out into the Pacific Ocean, a name which was an oxymoron to those sailors I had known who had sailed in the Sydney to

Hobart Yacht Race each December. It often became a survival course for even the most seasoned yachtsmen and in the past, several yachts had been sunk and there had also been several deaths at sea.

No! The Southern Pacific often not been very peaceful, at times but it got worse the further south one ventured. We would be soon coming down to the latitude of 40 degrees south, the home of the 'Roaring Forties', those strong and consistent westerly winds which had part of the southern route used by the old windjammers. They would come south from Europe then round the Cape of Good Hope at the southern tip of Africa, then race before the wind along the southern Indian Ocean before turning north to India and the Spice Islands. Some would continue along at their southern latitudes. being driven eastward by the winds - 'running the eastings down', as it was called, to sail below the southern shores of Australia before turning north to catch the Southeast Trade winds to the ports of Melbourne or Sydney. Many didn't make it and the Australian coast, west, south and east, contained the wreckage of many a ship.

Our course was luckily in the same direction as the prevailing north-westerly winds. These were also less severe than those of the 'Roaring Forties'. As we were on the lee side of southern island of New Zealand our voyage so far had been moderately comfortable.

Skipper had gone below but had soon returned with four cans of Speight's Larger. "Get that into you!" he said to Nobby at the wheel and then came up and sat on the top of the cabin opposite Mono and handed us each a can. "A great day to be sailing, eh?"

"Sweet" replied Mono, ripping the ring-pull of the can.

It was a great day; the wind was fresh enough, coming from behind us giving a comfortable sail and the early morning sun was warming us up after the cold of the night. I had always found that the Morning Watch was the best of all. It was sometimes a bit rugged being woken just before four in the morning; the cold and darkness only adding to the disorientation one felt at being woken in an unfamiliar bunk. But then one would see the sunrise with the light shining over a silver sea. That is, of course, if the weather was fine. In these waters, it was often not fine and one would come up onto a wet deck with the wind howling through the standing rigging and the sails luffing like mad as the previous watch-keeper struggled with the sheets which controlled them. Today was one of the better days for Morning Watch and so the entire crew was awake and looking forward to a good day's passage.

Skipper sucked on his can and looked at Mono. "So! How's the surveying business going, Mono?"

Mono tucked his can into the top of his life jacket and turned around. "Not as good as it was years ago. The Fossil Fuel Embargo put on shipping by the UN means that we only get smaller ships to survey these days. You know what it's like; a quick survey after they've refitted and then back to sea along some of the older coastal routes."

"Yeah! I know what you mean. We're getting fewer insurance jobs, too! As you say, the refitted vessels are only small, now. Not the huge super tankers and bulk carriers we use to get twenty year ago. Even the best storage batteries don't have the range unless the ships carry solar arrays. But then they limit deck space which is taken up by the containers so's the ships rely on short haul and overnight charging at the container wharfs. What do you think, Scotty?"

I put down my beer and brought my feet around into the cockpit. "Well, Skipper. Momo's right. The shipping industry has had to change since the amount of marine oil has been restricted. Still, I'm not complaining. Back home there's more work than I can handle designing new systems to convert the older diesel-electric engines to pure electric. The motors which control the screws and side thrusters are useable, but we have to reconnect them through their switching system to the banks of lithium-tungsten batteries."

"Sounds complicated," said Mono. "But at least they are less polluting that the old diesels."

"Well to some extent. The boffins[2] are still trying to work out the pollution caused by making the batteries and solar arrays."

"Yeah, well hopefully the reduction in the use of fossil fuels will slow down this global warming we have been experiencing. Our last summer in Enzed was almost as hot as your baked country 'Across the Ditch'[3], Scotty."

---

[2] Boffin – a Navy term for a scientist or anyone else who 'knows more than he should!'

[3] The Tasman Sea separating Australia from New Zealand.

Another sip on the can. "Well, you might be right there Mono, but we still have a few of the super ships about using gas turbines and there's some which have converted to use the new hydrogen fuels."

"Perhaps, Scotty. But I hear that the expense of conversion and the storage of such a volatile fuel probably makes their cargo fees too high. What do you think, Skipper, you're the insurance guy?"

Skipper wrapped the mainsheet around its cleat after letting it out a few more notches and gave Mono a big grin.

"Good for us, Mono! Too right! The cost of insuring H-ships as we call them has gone through the roof. I'm not sure that building even bigger ones will make up for the costs by economy of scale. The bigger they are, the more costly they are to insure and the risk also goes up, especially if they ply narrow entrances to ports."

Nobby at the wheel had been listening to the conversation in the cockpit. He was glad that his work was on land; it gave his imagination greater freedom to roam the world of the seafarers of past times. He took another suck on his beer and checked the GPS for any needed correction to their heading. Life was meant to be simple and each day enjoyed for what it was.

2.

Ship's Log of the Cetacean II*: 1000 hours Monday, 18th December, 2045. Position 39.12S, 176.42W; Winds moderate from the NW at 10 knots. Heading 168 degrees; Sky clear. A large ship under sail appeared on the horizon....*

It looked like another great day's sailing although the winds were still only moderate and abating. It was great to be alive! Mono had just taken over from Knobby on the wheel at the end of Morning Watch at 8 a.m. and Skipper was down below tidying up after breakfast in the galley when he noticed a bright dot on the small RADAR set which was still left on for night running. Knobby and I were enjoying our morning coffee stretched out on the cabin roof when Skipper called up from below.

"Hello! We've got a visitor." His head popped up through the open hatch and looked out to eastward, "Still about ten nautical miles off so we won't see her for a while. Big ship though." Skipper tended to use such distances such as Nautical Miles, believing that they were appropriate at sea, but the rest of us still though in terms of land-based distances unless we really had to use them.

"Rather strange for a big ship to be in these latitudes!" said Mono, who, as a Marine Surveyor had an interest in big ships and the routes that they plied.

"Yeah!" Skipper replied, leaning on the open hatch cover. "Nothin' much out here for good honest ships. Wop, Wops[4]. That's where we are!"

They were right, of course. We were on a very lonely part of the southwestern Pacific Ocean. I had done the last entry into our log and our GPS showed that we were about 400 kilometres north of Chatham Island. Nothing of the size that Skipper described from our RADAR would be in these waters.

Skipper went back into the main cabin and sat down at the cubby which held our radios, GPS unit and our little RADAR set. He fiddled with the dials of the unit mainly for something to do. He was interested in its new plot; anything out of the ordinary sea-going life of watching the sea, the sky and readjusting luffing sails. If we weren't lowering sails in a freshening wind, we were raising them in a light

---

[4] 'Wop wops' is New Zealand slang equivalent to the Australian 'woop woop' for 'middle of nowhere', an extremely remote place.

breeze. Knobby and I were content at the moment with just looking out at the sparking early morning sunlight glinting off the rolling green of the sea.

Below decks, Skipper continued to fiddle with our RADAR set in the hope of getting a better picture of our visitor. He called up the latest satellite image on SATVIEW, the best and latest replacement for Google Earth, and even if the definition was not the best for our part of the world, he managed to find a small, elongated shape which suggested a large vessel off to our east. A few adjustments to our RADAR showed that the large ship was on a parallel course to ours. Due south.

"Change course, Mono!" shouted Skipper from inside the cabin. "Bear 120 degrees. I'm curious to find out who she is. It's not often one runs into fellow travellers out here!"

"Aye, Aye, skipper" shouted Mono who often liked playing the 'old sea salt' and use such expressions.

Knobby had taken Skipper's high-powered binoculars and had stretched out on the foredeck, searching the horizon in front of our new course. It took some time before he turned and shouted:

"Ship on the horizon. I think she's a sailing ship!"
"Nonsense!" shouted Skipper who clambered over the cabin roof and knelt down beside the prone Nobby. Taking the glasses from him, he searched the horizon in the direction that Knobby was pointing.

"Well, I'll be…!" Skipper exclaimed. "You're right, Knobby! She is a sailing vessel; a big one at that. Come and have a look, Mono! Let Scotty take the wheel."

Mono went forward and took the binoculars from Skipper then re -focussed them for a clearer picture.

"What the hell is she doing here?"

"Do you know her, Mono?"

"Why yes. I think that it is the *Steelwind*."

"You've got to be joking! Let me have the glasses." Skipper steadied himself against the pulpit, the railing which went around the bow of the yacht. "You know! I think you're right! She shouldn't be here! The *Steelwind* is used mainly on the northern route out of Los Angeles bound for Asia on the Northeast Trades. She needs those winds and the

North Equatorial Current for her power! There's something greatly amiss for her to be this far south! Scotty, head towards her and let's find out what she's about."

Skipper, Mono and Knobby came aft and joined me in the cockpit. "What's the *Steelwind*?" Knobby asked as he had little real knowledge of world affairs.

Skipper ignored him for a moment and went below to fetch a pot of coffee which was brewing on his machine in the galley. He did like his coffee. He came back and settled himself on one of the cockpit's benches, handed out the mugs and poured out the coffee. Eventually, he put the pot down and looked at Knobby.

"Well, young Cornell," he said in a mock school-teacher voice. "The *Steelwind* is a bloody big sailing ship built only last year to carry trade across the Pacific. She's the brainchild of 'Dutch' Schmidt, the American billionaire shipbuilder who has more money than sense, I'm thinkin'."

Knobby looked past Skippers head, far out to the horizon where the upper sails of the ship in question had now become visible to the naked eye as a tiny speck. Skipper continued:

"Yeah! Well, our company had a chance to tender for her marine insurance like, so we got all of her details. Old Schmidt has a bit of a reputation as a forward thinker but also as someone who's also back in the past. His grandfather worked for the F. Laeisz Shipping company out of Hamburg in Germany – they made the big Flying P-liners; huge five-masted sailing ships including the *Preussen*. The *Steelwind* is modelled on that old square-rigger, but on a much bigger scale. The old *Preussen* was launched in 1902 for the Hamburg to South American nitrate trade. At a little over 8000 metric tons was the biggest sailor for all of that century. Unfortunately, she was wrecked in 1910 and soon the big steam ships took over. With the new fossil fuel moratorium by the UN, those big ships are also going to the breaker's yards. Too expensive to run on what little fuel is still around and big alternative electric and hydrogen-powered ships are also too expensive."

Skipper refilled his coffee cup as he looked out over the sea towards the speck on the far horizon. "It's a matter of power to weight ratio, you see, Knobby. Our current technology using lithium-titanium batteries and solar arrays can really only power small vessels. Most of the big diesel-electric super ships of over 300,000 metric tons have already been broken up. Even the smaller coastal ships have been beached unless they can be retrofitted to run on battery and solar power. The new hydrogen gas powered turbine ships have not yet got up to the size of their older predecessors as H-fuel is still hard to get and expensive. Old Schmidt thought to build a fleet of modern sailing ships to once again make use of free wind power but on a bigger scale – you know, over 10,000 tons or more. The *Steelwind* is twice the tonnage of the old *Preussen* but has all the mod cons as it were."

"But didn't they need hundreds of crews to sail these old windjammers?" asked Knobby who had read a few old 'Schoolboys Own' magazines about the days of fighting sail.

"Not now, matey!" replied Skipper. The old *Preussen* was modern for her day and only needed a crew of about forty. She had steam-powered winches, pumps, hoists and so on, so her crew hardly had to go aloft to furl and unfurl her huge sails. Steel-built too, she was with five big masts and over forty sails to match. She could do over twenty knots in a good following wind, that's more than the old super tankers could do. But I reckon that old Schmidt has got his knickers in a twist about the days of sail. Well, so our company thought too. We didn't think that bringing back big sailing ships was a good risk so we knocked back the tender."

"Bad decision!" Mono interrupted. "If you look at it from an economic point of view, it makes good sense. Wind is free, fuel oil is now too expensive or non-existent. We still need shipping in a big way. The Chinese are into building bigger H-fuel ships but they will still charge the earth for freight. A large fleet of sailing vessels over 10000 tons each could charge only a fraction of what the powered ships demand."

"Yeah nah!" Skipper retorted waving his hard across the mainsail of the *Cetacean II*; "sails are great if you have wind but pretty damn useless in a calm. Besides, you need some sort of power to get into tricky places or out of them when the wind turns rotten."

"Doesn't the *Steelwind* have auxiliary power?
"Well, yeah! She has good electric motors to drive two props at her stern and a couple of bow thrusters

as well, but they rely on batteries with solar arrays to recharge them during the day. Old Schmidt did come up with a bright idea and had his sails made up of strong, lightweight bamboo fibre coated with amorphous silicon to act as huge solar arrays, so there is plenty of power there but my company still thought the idea a bit too wacky."

"Sounds like the 'Old Men of the Sea' still have difficulty getting away from the concept of steam power. And nuclear-powered ships are not often welcome in many ports." Mono scoffed.

"Yeah, but at least a powered ship can go to any port she chooses and not rely on the wind."

"But hang on!" I butted into the heated conversation. "Weren't all of the great ports founded in the days of sail because they were at the ends or beginnings of the world's winds; Hong Kong, Singapore, Sydney, Auckland, western Europe, don't they all lie on the old trade routes"?

"He's right, you know Skipper," agreed Mono. "The *Steelwind* follows the old Spanish trading routes from California westward along the North Pacific Current with the Northeast Trade winds to Asia and then back to the States via the northern Pacific and its prevailing Westerlies. It makes a lot of sense to use the old trading routes, especially if your power source is free."

"Yeah, but they're still going to run into squalls and calms like they did in the old days. What then?"

Mono turned and gave me a cheeky wink. "The powered ships today still have some of those problems too, plus mechanical problems and the expense of fuel – if you can get it!"

"But what about crew, cargo space with all of that rigging and such?" chipped in Knobby.

"*Steelwind*" is designed to sail with a very small crew – under fifteen if I recall on the insurance tender. She is mostly controlled by an interactive computer system which handles all of the navigation and sail handling." Skipper finally conceded: "She has huge steel masts over 100 metres high which are engineered as part of the ship's complete hull structure so there is no standing rigging like on our little ship; no great ratlines for hundreds of topmen to go racing up to furl sail. Her booms on which the sails are attached are hinged where they join each mast and can also be raised and lowered for short distances. The sails are extendable out of these large-diameter booms and are furled or unfurled like giant window blinds, all controlled by the onboard computers. In a strong wind, they can be raised so only a part of their usual area is exposed depending on the ship's stability and wind speed; very much like we reef our mainsail if the wind gets up. The booms can also be rotated to take advantage of the prevailing winds so there is no need for cumbersome running rigging like we have to put up with. In port, all sails are taken up into their booms which are then hinged upward parallel to the mast which gives a clear space for access to the cargo, most of which is kept below decks in her huge hull spaces. She can take both small shipping containers below decks or can be quickly fitted out for bulk cargo."

It took sometime before Knobby could make out more detail of the *Steelwind* through Skipper's binoculars. "She looks a bit ragged, Skipper!" he said, passing the glasses over. Skipper steadied his arm on the cabin roof and took a good, long look.

"Crikey! You're right, Nobby. She looks in a bad way! Most of her sails are ripped and there are several booms hanging down by their masts. See if you can get her on the radio, Scotty!"

I dashed below and sat down at our radio desk. I had some experience in the use of radio during my army days and so I set the frequency at the Oceania region at 433 megahertz and called:

"*Steelwind, Steelwind.* This is the yacht *Cetacean II* on your starboard beam. Over."

Nothing but the slight hiss and static from the loudspeaker. I called again and then changed frequency to 2400MHz, a broadly accepted frequency around the world. I called again:

"*Steelwind, Steelwind.* This is the yacht *Cetacean II* on your starboard beam. Over." Again, nothing but hiss and static.

Finally, I tuned the set to several of the frequencies often used for distress signals and called again. Finally, having not received any reply, I tried Channel 16 at 156.8 MHz for short range maritime use and called again:

"*Steelwind, Steelwind.* This is the yacht *Cetacean II* on your starboard beam. Over." Again, nothing.

"*Steelwind, Steelwind.* This is the yacht *Cetacean II.* Nothing heard. Out," and left the radio on at the last channel and put the speaker onto 'open' so that we could monitor any further messages.

Going up on deck, I found my friends all looking towards the apparently stricken windjammer. Skipper turned around and looked at me with a grimace.

"Well, Scotty! It looks like she's been abandoned. No sign of any activity on deck and there's an accommodation ladder hanging down her side. Are you blokes game to board her?"

3.

Ship's Log of the Cetacean II: *1300 hours Tuesday, 19th December, 2045. Position 39.30S, 175.82W; Winds slight from the W at 5 knots. Heading 100 degrees; Sky clear. The* Steelwind *appearing to be abandoned, we decided to board her....*

Coming closer to the *Steelwind*, Skipper was able to give a better description of how she looked:

"Something amiss here!" he said, readjusting his binoculars "The accommodation ladder looks as if it has been smashed! Can't see anyone on deck and she looks like she hasn't been maintained." He put down the glasses. "Drop the sails, Mono. We'll motor in."

Knobby went below and lifted up the engine hatch in the floor of the cabin. Soon the comforting hum of our inboard electric marine engine filled the cabin. Knobby closed the hatch and came up into the cockpit. Skipper took the wheel as we motored towards the apparently abandoned vessel. Coming along side, we were awed at the size of the *Steelwind*; its huge silver-painted hull towered over us. Skipper carefully eased the little Cetacean II over to the damaged ladder and put our engine into neutral but kept it running.

"Momo, will you stay onboard while we three go to check her out? It looks a little sus to me so I may need you to get us away in a hurry."

"Right oh, Skipper!" he said, throwing a small line around one of the stays of the damaged accommodation ladder. "I'll put a slip knot to hold her for a quick getaway."

"O.K. lads. Are you with me?" he said. I could almost see him in some sort of 'pirate rig' with a cutlass in his mouth ready to board an enemy ship. But no, not today. Skipper carefully tested the stability of the small base platform of the ladder before he began to climb. Knobby followed and I took up the rear.

Through the small entry port in the three-strand wire safety railing which ran around the gunwale, we stepped up onto the deck of the *Steelwind* and looked around. The deck below the massive booms, cranes and sails was very spacious and relatively flat save for the small superstructures at the bow and stern of the ship and the large, rectangular hatch covers which took up most of the deck between the masts. There was no one in sight. The *Steelwind* did appear to have been abandoned. This was supported when Knobby pointed out the empty davits near the stern which would have held the ship's main lifeboat.

"Well, let's go forward and check out the bridge." Skipper said, turning towards the front of the ship. Unlike older sailing vessels, the *Steelwind* was steered and controlled by a low bridge superstructure just behind its bow. Two bridge wings came out from a central superstructure and small ladders came aft down to the deck. Like the hull, the superstructure was also painted silver.

"Rather a low bridge," I said to Skipper who looked up to the top of the foremast and said,

"No need for a high elevation as in the old super tankers, Scotty! Up there at the top of the forward mast is their RADAR platform and a high-definition camera fitted with telescopic lenses and with infra-red capabilities. One of the more positive features my company liked. The helmsman of the *Steelwind* only has to look at his monitors and he can see much further than by eye on a high bridge – and he can now see at night too."

Suddenly there was a loud whirring noise from behind us and above. One of the telescopic cranes was folding out from the mast. Its final position would be directly over the accommodation ladder and our small yacht. There was a huge pulley block with a large vicious hook attached to the cables at its end. Skipper looked up with some alarm and then ran back to the entry port in the side railing where we had entered. He yelled down to Mono who was standing in the bow of *Cetacean II* holding the loose end of the mooring line:

"Let go! For God's sake get away from the side!"

Mono looked up and saw the arm of the crane swinging out to be directly above the platform of the ladder and the bow of the yacht. He jerked the end of the mooring line and the bow of our little yacht swung out and away from the side of the platform. It was just in time. The big block and hook, now that its cables had been released, crashed down striking the railing of the yacht's pulpit a glancing blow before smashing into the ladder's platform. There was a loud, scraping noise as the bolts holding the upper platform of the accommodation ladder were wrenched out of the deck and the whole ladder slid down the side of the hull, just missing the yacht as it moved out away from the ship.

"Some bastard's out to get us!" Skipper swore aloud as he leant over the rail and cupped his hands around his mouth and yelled out to the yacht.

"Stand off some distance, Mono and try to keep up with us. We'll get off somehow!"

Mono had pulled himself up from the deck of the yacht where he had been thrown when the hook glanced off the pulpit rail. He stood up on the roof of the cabin and gave a wave of his arm before making his way aft to the cockpit.

Skipper hurried back to us with a look of determination on his weather-beaten face.

"Well, if someone's after our blood, then we have nowhere else to go but to look for the bastard." With that, he walked over to the side of the superstructure and wrenched a fire axe which had been loosely fastened to the bulkhead. "Up to the bridge, lads and remember that this ship has cameras and motion sensors everywhere and he probably knows our every move." He was pointing to a small, hemispherical glass object mounted just above where axe was located as he spoke.

We carefully climbed the ladder which went up to the narrow bridge wing on the forward superstructure. The door to the bridge was closed. Unlike most older ships, the outer doors of the superstructure, did not hinge outwards but slid sideways into internal recesses. Trying the handle, Skipper found that it was locked. He let it go and looked through the small glass port hole in the middle of the door. It was partly misted up but he turned to us with a look of horror on his face.

"I think that there's a body slumped over the control panel! Have a look."

Knobby went over to the port hole and looked in. He tried to wipe away some of the mist but it was all on the inside surface of the glass.

"Yeah! There's someone there all right and he looks like he's carked it!"

There was an emergency door release housed in a small, glass-faced red box not far from the right-hand edge of the door. Skipper smashed the glass with the handle of the fire axe and then pushed the red button inside the housing. There was a faint 'click' and the door gave a little vibration. Skipper once more tried the handle and the door slowly began to jerk open. There was a sudden hissing sound as gas was expelled through the narrow opening of the door.

"Gas!" Skipper yelled. "Probably carbon dioxide fire retardant from their Automatic Fire Extinguishing System (AFES). "Stand back!"

We all moved over to the forward railing of the bridge wing and waited until the gas stopped its noisy retreat from the bridge. Carbon dioxide gas is not only invisible but also odourless and fatal even at low percentages as it stops oxygen getting into the blood. This gas was certainly invisible but it was hot and had the foetid smell of death about it. When there was no audible sound of gas escaping, Skipper went back to the door and taking out his box of matches which he always carried along with his tobacco and pipe, lit a match and passed it through the narrow opening low to the deck. The flame immediately went out.

"Just as I thought! CO_2. It's both odourless, invisible and lethal above 5%. Anyone inside would have died pretty quickly when the bridge was flooded with the gas."

"Don't they have a warning alarm if there's a fire?" Knobby said.

"Usually. But that must have been overridden by the looks of the helmsman at the console. He certainly did get much of a chance to escape. We'll go around to the door on the other side and open it, too. That should get rid of most of the gas inside. But be careful, it is denser than air so it will hang around on the floor for some time."

We quickly ran down the ladder and around the front of the superstructure to the port side of the ship where there was another ladder to the bridge. Skipper repeated the opening of the door as before and then pushed the sliding hatch open as far as it could go. We would wait a few minutes in the hope that the through ventilation would expel most of the lethal gas inside.

Skipper cautiously stepped over the splash guard of the doorway as he entered the bridge. The helmsman was partly slumped over the small wheel on the wide console which ran the entire width of the bridge, had he had been dead for quite a while. The smell of his decay seemed to fill the cabin. Knobby called out from rear of the bridge:

"There's more stiffs over here!" he yelled.

Skipper and I left the dead helmsman and joined Knobby who was looking through a small door which opened into another cabin. There was a navigation chart, small table with a desk lamp as well as a single bunk. Probably the Captain's Day Cabin, I thought. Slumped over the desk was another body; the four rings on the sleeves of his jacket which had been hung over the back of the chair showed that the body was that of the Captain of the *Steelwind*. Further inside the cabin, another body lay on the floor. The three rings on his epaulettes showed that he was the First Officer.

Skipper covered the bodies up with sheets from the bunk, he also took a blanket out to cover the body of the helmsman whom Knobby had laid down on the floor of the bridge. Skipper made the sign of the cross over the two bodies in the cabin. He was not a particularly religious man and swore with the best of them but this too, was part of his seafaring image. "There's another door here!" said Knobby, pointing to a closed door in the rear bulkhead of the bridge a little way between the Captain's Day Cabin and the port entrance. It was a more traditional door which hinged outward.

Careful!" warned Skipper. "Remember that there is probably a murderer onboard somewhere. We don't know where he is but I'm certain that he knows where we are! Here's the axe. Keep an eye on that door's latch and give us a yell if you see it move." He turned to me. "Scotty, you've got to be the lookout for both bridge doorways. I want to keep them open so that this gas can be cleared. I'm going to check out the Voicelog in the Captain's cabin."

With that, Skipper returned to the Captain's Day Cabin and went up to the Voicelog which was above the small desk. A low hum from it showed that it was still recording. He switched it off and then back on again.

Voicelogs are as much a feature of commercial shipping and some larger private vessels as the

Black Box Recorders (BBR) are to large aircraft. They serve both the role of a BBR and a verbal edition of a traditional ship's log. Unlike Skipper's traditional paper log aboard the *Cetacean II*, a Voicelog is more like a Dictaphone, which takes down the verbal comments of its subscriber and records it on a continuous wire loop. Pressing the ON button also automatically detects input from the several shipboard sensors, the main computer and gives the usual location coordinates, time, date, ship's speed and direction as well as the sea and wind conditions and the temperature. This information from previous logs can be accessed by simply using the rewind and play buttons on the device. When a log is replayed it is displayed on the small screen as text. Skipper rewound the log, finding several disturbing entries and then a sudden cessation of logs. The last entry was dated several weeks ago.

4.

Voicelog of the Steelwind: *0900 hours Friday, November 25, 2044. Position 001.87N, 155.93W six days out of port and nearing the island of Kiritimati; Winds slight from the E at 5 knots. Heading 270 degrees; Sky clear. Outside temperature 35 degrees Celsius and our air conditioning unit has broken down again. Mr. Hobbs, our Computer Officer has made yet another formal complaint about the probable harmful effects of the high temperature our computer. His behaviour has become even more erratic...*

Skipper read the text on the small red screen for the entry where the tragedy of the *Steelwind* seemed to have started. He looked at the map on the bulkhead above the desk showing the extensive Pacific Ocean and noted the inked-in course of the ship between its home port of Los Angeles and its destination of Tokyo. The *Steelwind* had sailed southwest down the Californian coast along the California Current with the North East Trade winds behind her until she caught the North Equatorial Current flowing westward. The planned course would have taken her well to the west until she reached the Kuroshio Current at about 140 East Latitude when she would have turned north to sail to her final destination. Unfortunately, subsequent logs showed otherwise.

Skipper fast forwarded and quickly read on the screen several mundane entries as the *Steelwind* approached the island of Kiritimati in the Kiribati group then stopped and played another entry:

Voicelog of the Steelwind*: 1400 hours Saturday, November 26, 2044. Position 001.97N, 157.49W anchored offshore on the western side of the island of Kiritimati out from the northern passage to the lagoon; Sheltered position with light Sky overcast. Outside temperature 33 degrees Celsius. An accident occurred as the Kiribati Customs Officer came aboard. The crane above the accommodation ladder suddenly swung out and dropped its hook onto the boarding platform just missing the officer. I was then informed that the* Steelwind *should remain anchored offshore until further investigations were made about this incident....*

"So, this was no accident even then." Skipper said aloud. "Whoever did this obviously did not want visitors on board the ship!" He forwarded the log on to the next day to see the result of any investigation that the *Steelwind's* Captain recorded:

Voicelog of the Steelwind*: 0800 hours Sunday, November 27, 2044. Position 001.97N, 157.49W anchored offshore on the western side of the island of*

Kiritimati out from the northern passage to the lagoon; Sheltered position with light Sky overcast. Outside temperature 29 degrees Celsius. It being Sunday, crew set to 'make-and-mend'. Engineer McIntosh detailed to look into the matter of the defective crane....

Another entry later that day at 1300 hours:

.... Engineer McIntosh reported that he could find no mechanical cause for the crane to fail. No cooperation from Mr. Hobbs, the Computer Officer who has locked the cabin door to the Computer Cabin and did not respond to Mr. McIntosh's requests to allow access to his computer systems. McIntosh has asked permission to allow the computer cabin be accessed despite Mr. Hobbs's objections. No response from Mr. Hobbs to this request so I thought it advisable for the time being to allow Mr. Hobbs to think over the matter....

However, the next log showed that this decision had been a fatal error of judgement:

Voicelog of the Steelwind: *2000 hours Sunday, November 27, 2044. Position 001.97N, 157.49W anchored offshore on the western side of the island of Kiritimati out from the northern passage to the lagoon; Sheltered position with light Skies clearing. Outside temperature 32 degrees Celsius. Engineer McIntosh did not attend the usual daily meeting after the evening meal in the Officer's Wardroom. Steward Ward was sent to request the Engineer's presence but reported back, very distressed that he opened the cabin door he found the Engineer dead in his cabin and the room full of gas from the AFES which had been activated. It should be noted in this log that such an event may not have been an accident...*

Skipper read this log entry with some conviction that the death of the engineer certainly was no accident. The next few entries of the log showed that the Captain was obviously distressed at this second 'accident'. Members of the crew were detailed to remove the body of the engineer but were reluctant to do so. They were able to complete the task using respirators from the fire locker. It was decided to keep the door locked until the authorities from the island could come on board and look into the matter; the ship now being in Kiribati waters. Another entry the next day:

Voicelog of the Steelwind: *0800 hours Monday, November 28, 2044. Position 001.97N, 157.49W anchored offshore on the western side of the island of Kiritimati out from the northern passage to the lagoon;*

With a long voyage in front of them, the Captain's
next log entry later that morning was alarming:

This entry explained the missing lifeboat and the
damaged accommodation ladder but the next part of
this log still left many questions unanswered:

controls, Mr. Weatherby the First Officer and I decided to confront Mr. Hobbs and have him override the computer controls. This may mean breaking into his cabin and....

There was the low hum from the Voicelog as before showing that this entry was the last that the Captain had made. Skipper was concerned many things could have happened since that last entry for last November, over three weeks ago. Mr. Hobbs, the Computing Officer had obviously gone mad and has manipulated his computer to kill off anyone who would interfere with his need to turn the ship to the south. But why? There was nothing between the island of Kiritimati and Antarctic but thousands of kilometres of the wild seas of the Southern Ocean. Suddenly an unpleasant though hit home. The Southern Ocean and Antarctica! With little joy from the Engineer and the Captain's plan to head further north and with the air conditioning unit damaged, there would be a very strong possibility that the main computer would suffer even more damage from the heat. In fact, if one could think of the computer as a living entity as a living entity, it was dying and knew it. Mr. Hobbs was obviously one of those computer types who had a very personal relationship with his computer, above all that he had with other humans. It must be protected at all costs.

Mr Hobbs was now confirmed in Skipper's mind as their main adversary on board *Steelwind* and that his life and that of his two friends depended upon finding Mr. Hobbs and putting an end to his murderous activities. Skipper came out of the Captain's Day Cabin and said:

"Look, lads! It's this Mr. Hobbs the Computer Officer who is out to get us like he did with these three poor blokes. We're going to have to find him and lock him up and take over the ship. Are you up to handling a big, modern computer Scotty?"

I looked at Skipper with some degree of alarm. Tackling a murderer on his own ship would be hard enough but then also taking on his computer was another problem. I thought for a while and then gave him my answer:

"Well, my company's mainframe is not the current generation of AI[1] computers, but I have tried to keep up with modern trends. It would depend on how this Mr. Hobbs has programmed and modified it. Remember that this computer probably has considerable independence so that it can read the

---

[1] AI – Artificial Intelligence, computer programming to give some human comprehension and freedom of action

weather and sea conditions then operate all of the booms, sails and other paraphernalia needed to sail such a ship as this. I would have to log into the computer's program and see how it all works before trying to reverse any course headings and of course, override the fire extinguishers and cranes."

"Good man!" Skipper said, picked up the fire axe and went over to a schematic of the ship's structure on the rear bulkhead. "This is a 'Two-island' design, it has another deck house in the stern as well as this bridge superstructure. "Look here!" he said, pointing to a section of the plan of the large deckhouse at the ship's stern. "The computer cabin is located at the stern, probably so that Mr. Hobbs could see how his beloved computer was handling the sails and such. That is where we will find our man. But let's take all care! The man's a nutter."

We followed Skipper out of the bridge and down the ladder to the main deck. "Keep your eyes peeled, lads! There are sensors and cameras everywhere and all manner of ways that Hobbs can do us an injury. Watch out above Knobby. That's your job. A falling pulley block on steel cable would do the trick. Scotty, you look out for any potential attacks on the deck, steam pipes, electrical cables and the like. Follow me."

We walked along the port side deck close to the railing, apprehensive that at any moment Hobbs would spring another unknown attack on us. We could not see any sign of our little *Cetacean II* and hoped that Mono was able to single sail the yacht. Finally, we came to the rear deckhouse which was not unlike the one we had left. Skipper was right. Whilst only a single story, it did have a bank of windows along the front and front roof which would give an ample view of the ship's sail plan as well as the deck.

The door in the side of the port bulkhead closest to the windows was locked but Skipper again smashed the glass of the emergency lock and was able to slowly slide the door open. Again, there was a rush of heated gas from the interior.

"The bastard's not taking any chances, is he?" said Skipper standing back from the door which we could see opened into a companionway which ran down the side of the deck house.

After a short time, Skipper lit another match and held it through the door at about waist height. The flame flicked a bit but remained alight showing that the carbon dioxide level had sunk to the floor.

"OK. Watch yourselves! Anything can happen now." Skipper said, cautiously stepping over the threshold and entering the companionway. To our right, it opened out into what appeared to be an observation and control room with the glass windows taking up much of the forward bulkhead. "The main computer room must be down to the left."

We slowly walked down the narrow companionway, our eyes everywhere expecting some madman to suddenly rush out of a door or even from where we had just been. Skipper now had the fire axe raised across his chest ready for anything.

The was a door now in the inner bulkhead with the words COMPUTER ROOM – ACCESS RESTRICTED written in large letters below a small porthole. Skipper looked in but again, the glass was fogged. He tried the door latch and as expected, it too was locked.

"I'm going to unlock the door with the emergency button but I will have to use the axe to lever it aside so watch out. This loony may take a rush for the door or he may even be armed."

With that, Skipper repeated his 'break-and-entry' procedure to open the computer rooms door. We all thought that Hobbs would have disabled most of the hull and interior cabins using the fire prevention system and would have left his part of the ship safe. As the door slowly slide sideways, there again was the unforgettable hiss of warm gas and the foetid smell of death.

5.

Diary of Computer Officer Class 1 Justin Hobbs: 1:30 pm., Saturday, November 26, 2044. We have just anchored off the island of Kiritimati and I am convinced that the captain is going to do something extreme to get this heat under control. CONI[1] is not behaving as she should be because of the heat affecting her circuits. I have done my best by turning on fans and opening doors but that is not much help in these confounded tropics. I must keep the captain from disabling CONI's operations. She still retails some voice activation but I fear that if the temperature gets too high, she may activate her self-defence sub-routine. I will attempt to re-program that sub-routine and bring CONI down to manual control.

We entered the cabin after a short wait and found the body of a man on the floor not far from the computer keyboard. The diary on his small desk near the door was written in ink in a spidery scrawl and it seemed that Mr. Hobbs did not trust voicelogs or any other electronic recording systems connected to his computer. There were some things on his mind that he preferred to record in the old style of ink and paper. Over on the other bulkhead, far

---

[1] CONI – Computer Operated Navigation & Instruments; the *Steelwind's* main computer.

across the wide room was the main computer and its banks of memory slots, dials, lights and a large keyboard positioned just below a large monitor set into the main structure. Mr Hobbs – our suspected murderer had himself been murdered. By the computer.

We looked at each other in surprise. Skipper turned to me and said: "It looks like Mr. Hobbs had the same idea as us; to de-activate the computer but he obviously was not in time. That dated entry was on the same day as CONI tried to stop the officials from the island coming on board. Can you do anything, Scotty?"

"I'll try!" I said, walking over to the keyboard and sat down in the chair. Luckily there was no other close-hand defence mechanism such as electrification of the chair or keyboard, so I sat down at the keyboard and pressed ENTER. Initially there was no response, but then the monitor lit up with the company's logo and the words' Computer Operated Navigation & Instruments' slowly undissolved onto the screen. Suddenly, a very smooth-sounding female voice came over the stereo loud speakers above and on either side of the keyboard was heard:

"Hello. I am CONI. How may help?"

So, no password was needed to open the computer. Hobbs probably relied on the security of the computer room and his own personal presence to prevent any tampering with his beloved computer. I sat for a while and then said aloud:

"CONI will you open your self-defence subroutine on the monitor, please?" I had always believed that talking to computers and cell phones to be a degree of social foolishness and self-indulgence. I remembered my early days as an undergraduate computer studies student at university and having to use some of the older voice-activated programs. We often had a lot of fun using 'tongue-twisters' and nonsense words to see what the computer response would be. In those days, one had to speak very clearly and in words with distinct syllables – much like the caricatures of nervous policemen giving evidence in court. We would laugh when some external sound would also be detected on our sensitive microphones and be incorporated into the program or aps which were being created. Here was another entirely different situation. CONI had obviously been built and programmed with a sophisticated level of AI and it had a lethal understanding by way of the many sensors around the ship of how to protect itself.

The female voice from the computer replied:

"I am sorry Guest. You do not have access to this subroutine. Please enter the password."

A dialogue box opened at the bottom of the screen for me to enter a password. But what could it be? I entered several of the most obvious passwords from 12345678 to QWERTY12 and felt foolish doing so. A man like Hobbs would not have such a simplistic password. I entered STEELWIND and several other passwords connected to the ship, her company and the sea; all with no result. There was no option such as one often gets on a PC to reset the password. Then, suddenly a flashing message appeared on the screen:

TIME EXPIRY IN 10 SECONDS and the numbers began to count down from 10.

I tried everything that I knew to bypass the password entry. I went into the RUN command and get the Command Prompt to manually override the password by rewriting the password subroutine. Nothing would work. Finally, the last digit came up and the screen went red and the warning text scrolled down:

DANGER: SELF DEFENCE MECHANISMS ACTIVATED.

Luckily Skipper was watching my attempts to override with CONI carefully and when he heard a click behind him, he was able to quickly jam the fire axe he still carried into the door's threshold as it began to slide shut. There was an ominous hissing sound from the valves in the ceiling as the Automatic Fire Extinguishing System began to stream the lethal gas into the cabin.

"Quick! Let's get out of here before the other doors close," he said. Knobby and I quickly followed him out through the door and Knobby was just in time to stop the outer door from closing shut.

Back on the deck, we found that the sun had set and night was rapidly upon us. We were alarmed the see the nearest crane begin to extend out from the stern mast and swing above us.

"Back to the stern rail, hurry!" Skipper called as he ran back to the very stern of the ship. We followed close behind and so did the swinging crane boom; its big pulley and hook block suddenly crashing down on the deck just behind us. Skipper looked up and smashed a glass bulb which contained a security camera.

"That should slow her down for a while!" he cried in triumph but this was short-lived as the big boom of the spanker, that large fore-and-aft sail at the very stern of the ship began to swing from one side to another like a blind man swing his cane. Suddenly, as though frustrated with its ineffectual operation, it crashed down onto the top of the deckhouse.

We had little to fear from this boom as the stern deckhouse was below it which protected us from its cleaving motion. Skipper ran to one of the white cylindrical life raft cannisters which sat in its cradle on the gun'le and used the axe to lever it off.

"Quick! Let's get this open and over the side. Knobby, there's a loose coil of rope hanging from the end of the spanker boom. Cut it off and bring it here." With that, he threw the axe to Knobby who caught it mid-air and began to hack the long length of rope off the boom.

Skipper rolled the life raft cannister onto the deck. "Damn!" he said. "It has a hydrostatic valve attached."

"What's that?" I said in innocence.

"It's a valve which opens the cannister only when the ship has sunk for a few metres. The water pressure then pulls the cable out of the cannister and opens it up so that the life raft can inflate."

"But how do we get it to inflate if we are not sinking?"

"Easy!" he said turning to Knobby. "Give us the axe again mate!" Knobby threw the axe back to Skipper who then broke the fitting which held the hydrostatic release unit (HRU) to the frame of the ship. Grasping it firmly, he sat down on the deck and put both feet on the cannister so that the HRU was between his legs. He slowly began to pull the rope cable out of its cannister until he felt some resistance. Relaxing his arms and bending his knees, he pulled the rope suddenly with all of his strength. There was a small popping sound and the hinged cannister split in two; the mass of the life raft began to emerge from its cannister like some giant, obscene orange slug. "Come on! Help me stand this thing up against the bulkhead before it falls over the railing!"

Knobby and I ran to help Skipper who was now trying desperately to move the large, inflating life raft up onto its leading edge so that it would stand sideways on the deck. He grabbed the coil of rope from Knobby and fastened one end of it to a railing stanchion and the other end to a large, black plastic eyelet on the raft. Luckily it was a 6-man life raft weighing only about thirty kilograms. We lifted the bulky raft over the railing and let it slip down the side of the *Steelwind's* hull. It hit the water with a splash and drifted only a short way from the hull thanks to the length of the rope which Knobby had obtained. Skipper hauled in the slack so that the life raft was now up against the hull.

"Right-oh! Over youse go!" he said with a gleam in his eye.

I went first, having had some experience with rock climbing near my native Sydney. Down I went with my feet on the hull and my legs pushed out until I felt the edge of the life raft and then dropped through its opening into the security of its dry interior. A rather ungainly Knobby followed and almost fell into the sea before I grabbed his jacket and pulled him into the life raft. Skipper soon dropped down beside us and set about untying the raft from the rope. I expected at any moment that a heavy pulley block would drop and crush our small life raft but luckily it still lay on the deck above us where it had tried to kill us before.

We drifted away from the *Steelwind's* hull and for the first time felt safe, even though we were now adrift on a vast and lonely stretch of dark ocean a long way from anywhere. *Steelwind* continued in its slow course southward.

Skipper rummaged through the large utility bag fastened to the inside of the raft and pulled out its contents. He soon found a small waterproof flashlight and spread the contents out onto the undulating floor. There were several useful items in the kit as well as the flashlight. These included: two red hand flares; a hand bailer; Signal mirror; repair kit; whistle and two small paddles. There was no emergency food nor water and we could feel that the wind was getting up and the sea was beginning to roll. Night had fallen and the air inside the hood of the raft was cold and damp.

We drifted for some time before Knobby let out a shout: "Look! There's a light!"

We all rushed over to the small opening and saw a faint white light through the gloom.

"It's got to be the Cetacean II!" cried the Skipper who reached down into the bag and pulled out one of the hand-held red flares. He extended his arm out as far as it would go and pulled the flare's yellow tag. In a few seconds it burst into life with a red flash and sparks flying down onto the water. Soon the flare went out but Skipper grabbed the flashlight and waved it back and forth. We were overjoyed when we saw a smaller white light repeating this motion from the yacht.

It took some time after the flare had gone out before we saw the welcome sight of our small yacht's bow slowly emerging from the night's gloom. Mono manoeuvred the yacht so that the raft was at the stern so we were able to clamber awkwardly into its cockpit. Mono gave us a broad grin to hide his relief:

"What took you so long? I thought that I was going to have to do a lone hand voyage."

We all laughed at his welcome and after a short while, with a mug of steaming cocoa in my hand, I looked out over the darkening sea and wondered about the potential of a fleet of large sailing vessels which could solve the world's transportation problems in a new world without fossil fuels. I also wondered about the fate of the *Steelwind*.

Epilogue

Log of Ice Reconnaissance Team Delta, USAP[1]: Friday, February 10, 2045, 1600 hours. Position: -60.31, -172.80. On route from S/V Lincoln Ellsworth *to the edge of the ice sheet, Ross Sea. Winds 10 knots from the west. Sky clear.*

The large orange hovercopter skimmed low over the edge of the seemingly endless sea of white ice and the grey sea. The quiet hum of its two large ducted fan electric motors filled the cabin whilst the co-pilot scanned the northern horizon for the open sea. There were only three persons on board: Dr. Harper Sinclair, the program's glaciologist; Sam Carter, the pilot and Juan Rodriquez his co-pilot.

"Can't see a blasted thing in this white glare!" The co-pilot swore before lowering the grey visor of his flying helmet.

"Ah, c'mon, Juan! You could spot a snowman wearing a white suit in a blizzard!" teased Dr. Sinclair who had been with this team on several trips out to plot the edge of the ice sheet this season in the Ross Sea.

---

[1] USAP – United States Antarctic Program.

They had taken off from the *Lincoln Ellsworth* early that morning and now were heading west along the edge of the ice sheet. Dr. Harper had predicted that the Ross Sea ice sheet would have shrunk by over 25% due to the current increase in global temperature.

"What tha'!" shouted the co-pilot who was hurriedly adjusting the focus on his binoculars. "Ah don't believe it! Will ya look over yonder'!" he said pointing a little to the right and down at the ice. "If ah didn't know any betta, ah would swear that there's a big sailing ship down there in the ice! Swing her around, Sam."

Sam swung the big hovercover in a tight turn then dropped down about another hundred feet. Dr. Sinclair came up and crouched behind the co-pilot's seat and looked out over his shoulder as they flew over what appeared to be a large windjammer stuck in the ice. It was situated only about a few hundred yards from the edge of the ice sheet where it was at its thinnest.

"Can you put her down, Sam?" said Dr. Sinclair.

"Sure thing, Doc! Just hang on in case we hit a patch of soft snow over the ice."

Sam landed the hovercopter on a flat section of hard snow about twenty yards from the ship which now loomed large over the aircraft. He cut the motors and turned around in his seat.

"Darndest thing I ever saw in the ice, Doc! It almost looks like one of them photos from books about the early explorers. I better get back to the LE[2] and tell'em about this.

"Yes, go for it, Sam. Good idea. We should investigate this but I'd like the boys back on our ship to know what we are getting up to."

Sam plucked the handset from the radio console in the control panel and started to broadcast:

"*Lincoln Ellsworth,* this is Ice Team Delta. Over"

There was a slight crackle from the loudspeaker, then the cheery voice of 'Tex' Connor, the *Lincoln Ellsworth's* Radio Operator:

---

[2] LE – his slang term for the Research Vessel *Lincoln Ellsworth.*

"Well, hi ya, Sam. How are doin'?"

"Fine, Tex. Hey listen. You'll not believe what we've just found out here on the edge!"

"What, you've found an alien flying like them tha' conspiracy boys are always talkin' about?"

"No, I'm serious Tex. It's like goin' back in time. We've done found a big windjammer. You know! A darned big sailing ship like in the history books. Big hull and five big masts towering over us."

"Where the Hell are ya, Sam?"

"We're on the ice and sittin' about twenty yards off her. She's big alright. Doc wants to check her out."

"Hang on, Sam. I'll see the boss about that. Wait Out." There was silence from the loud speaker and Sam turned around to look at his two companions. "Do we really want to go aboard her? She looks like a ghost ship to me with all of that rigging covered in ice and them snow drifts right up to her deck."

"Sure do, Sam." Said Dr. Sinclair. "It doesn't look like a ghost ship to me. She's too modern. Look at those masts! All steel if I'm not mistaken. And what's left of the sails looks like some type of solar array. I remember hearing that some outfit in LA was going to build such a ship."

The loudspeaker crackled back into life: *"Lincoln Ellsworth to Ice Team Delta. Over."*

"I hear ya loud and clear, Tex. What did the boss have to say?"

"Yeah, Sam. Go ahead but watch what ya all are doin' Ya never know what ya might find. QTX[3]

"Roger that, Tex. We'll patch our handsets to this set so you can hear us at all times. We'll give ya a runnin' commentary of our ghost ship adventures."

Sam took out three small handsets from a locker below the radio console then dialled in a frequency which would link the operators to be relayed directly to the *Lincoln Ellsworth*. "All set, Doc." He said handing the small radios to his companions.

-----

[3] Radio term for "Will you keep your station open for further communication with me? I will keep my station open for further communication with you."

"Right, guys! Suit up for some cold weather."

Putting on their heavy thermal over suits with their fur-lined hoods, the three left the hovercopter and carefully walked towards the ship embedded in the ice. Sam led, using a pole to check the snow for any crevasse or crack in the ice below. There was one particular snow drift which went almost up to the side of the ship near what looked like a command superstructure. Climbing over an ice-covered rail, the three carefully climbed up the icy steps of the ladder which led to the starboard bridge wing. They were surprised to see that the door was open so they carefully entered.

The bridge deckhead and bulkheads[4] were covered with ice as was most of the deck and there were small snow drifts inside both doorways. Long icicles hung from the deckhead and most of the glass windows.

"Oh gosh!" said Juan. "We've got some bodies here! Three of them!" he said with alarm pointing to three icy forms lying in the centre of the cabin, covered with a thick layer of transparent ice.

---

[4] Deckhead – ceiling; bulkheads-walls

Dr. Sinclair went over the slippery deck kneeling down to look at the three shapes.

"It seems like someone else has been here. Look! They have been covered with blankets. Nothing more here, let's take a look at the other superstructure down at the end of the ship."

She brought her handset up to her mouth:

"Hello Tex? Can you hear me."

"Loud an' clear, Doc!" came the quick response.

"Tex, tell the boss that we've got three bodies on this ship which seems deserted."

"Roger that, Doc. By-the-way, the boss is here and he thinks that the ship is the *Steelwind*. It was last seen off Kiribati near the equator and has been listed as 'missing'.

"Thanks, Tex. We are going to the back of the ship to see if there's anyone else in the other section. See you soon. Listen in."

"Roger, Doc. I'll be here."

Dr. Sinclair led her three companions along the slippery snow and ice-covered deck of the *Steelwind*. There was a moderate wind blowing through the tangled cables and strips of sails hanging down from the masts and booms above. Some of the cranes attached to the masts hung out at various angles and the long boom at the rear of the ship had fallen down onto the roof of the rear superstructure.

Here, they found that the outer door was closed, but Juan managed to unlatch it using the red emergency button in its broken casing on the wall. He used a fire axe, which he found embedded in ice on top of the roof of the low building and managed to lever the door open.

Inside, the corridor was relatively free of ice. Its dark walls glistened with crystals and there were a few larger stalactites of ice down some of the internal pipes. It seemed that this part of the ship had been heated for a while at least. Sam took out his cell phone and opened the Spotlight app. There was another closed door just along the corridor to the right. Juan again used the emergency button and axe to open the door.

Inside the darkened room, there was little evidence of ice save for a light covering of crystals on the wall which sparkled when Sam shone his light around the walls.

"It's the computer room!" said Sam. "We may be able to fire her up and see what went on here. It looks like the Voicelog over yonder has been dismantled...oh say, look! There's another deadun over there!" he said pointing to the body which lay further over to one side. Unlike the others in the bridge, this one was simply covered in a thin frosting of ice and they could see from his uniform that he was one of the ship's officers.

"Leave him be, Sam." Dr. Sinclair said. "It looks like there's no power here. How can you fire up the computer, Sam?"

"Easy, Doc! I'll get a power pack from the hovercopter. You know, the ones we use to wake up some of the snowcats back at McMurdo. Back in a while." With that he went out of the cabin.

Juan and Dr. Sinclair looked around the cabin. Apart from the body and the surface ice crystals, it looked fairly ordinary. On examination, the body seemed to have been dead for some time. She thought in a grim way that he wasn't going to deteriorate much in this cold.

Sam soon returned carrying the large backpack which contained the powerful fully charged lithium battery which was used to start up cold vehicles and aircraft back at the the shore base of McMurdo Station well to the south.

"Hey, Doc! I noticed when I was coming back that she's lost her lifeboat and at least one life raft. Perhaps tha crew musta got off at some stage. Well, let's plug her in and see if we can't fire this baby up!"

Sam undid the electrical cables with their huge clips from the backpack and rummaged around in several of the hatches in the front of the huge computer. Finally, he stood up and said with some pride:

"There she be! All hooked up. Now let's see what this baby will do."

He pressed the activation switch and there was a slight humming sound as the electricity flowed into the computer. Some of the lights blinked on and soon the large monitor lit up with the company's logo and the words' Computer Operated Navigation & Instruments' slowly undissolved onto the screen. Then a very faint female voice came over the stereo loud speakers above and on either side of the keyboard was heard:

"Hello. I am CONI. How may help?"

Dr. Sinclair was momentarily taken back, but recovered her senses and spoke to the computer:

"Umm…hello. Can we give verbal commands to you?"

The computer spoke again in its soft, reassuring female voice: "I am sorry Guest. You do not have access. Please enter the password." The screen went black and a password command window opened.

Dr. Sinclair looked blankly around at her colleagues who now stood in front of the computer. "Any ideas?"

"Not a clue," said Sam. Juan just shook his head.

After a few moments of inaction, a flashing message appeared on the screen:

TIME EXPIRY IN 10 SECONDS and the numbers began to count down from 10.

10 – 9 - 8 - 7- 6 – 5 -4 - 3 - 2 -1

Finally, the when last digit disappeared from the screen it suddenly went red and the warning text scrolled down:

DANGER: SELF DEFENCE MECHANISMS ACTIVATED.

A voice came over the handset which now lay on the floor:

"Hello, Ice Team Delta. Do you read me? Come in."

It was repeated:

"Hello, Ice Team Delta. Do you read me? Come in."

"Hello, Doc? Sam? Juan? Can you hear me?"

There was no response. Outside the wind blew cold
and hard.

About the Author

Peter Scott was born and raised in Sydney and has written over twenty books including non-fiction on Earth Science, the environment, survival and teaching. In the last few years, he has turned to fiction and has written in a variety of genres, mainly historical adventure and science friction. Graduating from Sydney Teachers' College as a teacher of Middle School Science at the age of nineteen, he later completed part-time studies gaining a Bachelor of Science, Masters Degrees in Science and Educational Administration and finally a Doctorate in Education. He has taught in both schools and University. During this time, he married and raised a family as well as serving as a Commissioned Officer in the Army Reserve and later an Officer/Instructor and Commanding Officer of an Australian Naval Cadet unit. With some minor sea experience with the Royal Australian Navy, he had six training cruises at sea on board 'Tall Ships', both square- and schooner-rigged. Having travelled extensively to all seven continents, including Antarctica, he has always followed his interests and so his novels often reflect his personal experiences.

Other Books by the Author

Fiction

Tom Shipley Series (Humour)

The Innocence of Tom Shipley: Teacher. A 19-year-old teacher reports to his first school to find that he is the Acting Head of Department. He meets many interesting characters in his first years of teaching.

Tom Shipley's War, Memoirs of a Weekend Warrior. 1965 and the first ballot for Australian conscripts for the Vietnam War. With many of his friends drafted and the protest movement now directed against them, Tom Shipley enlists into the local Army Reserve unit and finds a new enemy; the Army itself.

Tall Ships Series (Historical Science Fiction)

The Ice Ship. 1840 and an advanced steam-auxiliary whaling ship sets out from New England to go whaling in Antarctic waters. A freak storm of cold weather sends it further south and it becomes embedded in the ice.

Panicked, the crew desert and leave their young captain on board. This is a tale about their survival.

Two Hundred Years before the Mast, An Adventure in Time. It is 1996 and a young Nuclear Physicist accidently discovers how to travel in time. Having an interest in the days of fighting sail, he goes back to the year 1796 where he is unexpectedly press ganged aboard a Royal Navy frigate. How does he survive the peril in which his ship is placed?

<u>**San Rafael Series**</u> **(Historical Adventure -written as 'Hernan Moreno Ruiz')**

Letters from San Rafael. It is 1880 and Peruvian intelligence officer, Colonel Moreno and his Sergeant, Garcia, are captured by the Ecuadorians during a border dispute and taken to the supply depot of San Rafael in Ecuador. Treated as guests by the old Comandante, Moreno is able to smuggle letters home. They each tell a separate tale about South America and its people at that time as told to Morano by the people of San Rafael.

Return to San Rafael. Ten years on and Moreno and Garcia are called upon by their former captors to return to the now deserted hacienda of San Rafael to discover its secret which will affect the future of both Peru and Ecuador. Along the way they hear many stories of the places through which they travel and meet the mysterious Father Xavier, a Jesuit priest who knows more about their secret mission than they do.

Confessions of Father Xavier. Set in the 1870's, this is the story of how a young Peruvian cavalry officer becomes the mysterious Jesuit priest, Father Xavier and the many adventures he has before becoming an agent for both the Church and Government.

<u>Australian Bush Stories</u> (Short Stories)

Cry of the Currawong. A series of short, connected and humorous stories about Australian country life in the 1950's and how a young boy from the city finds many adventures with his new-found cousins, uncles and aunts.

Non-Fiction

Survival Series

A Pocketbook of Hiking and Survival. A pocket encyclopaedia of survival skills for the outdoors designed to be carried in pocket or pack.

A Pocketbook of Surviving Teaching and Instruction. A guide for all teachers and instructors, sometimes in a humorous vein, based on over 40 years of experience in teaching and instruction.

Surviving Global Warming: A Guide for the Future. A complete guide to climate change both natural and man-made with special reference to resources and energy. Each chapter has a personal how to survive section.

Adventures in Earth Science Series

Adventures in Earth Science (compendium issue). A complete encyclopaedia about the Earth and beyond written with over 40 years of experience and travels on all seven continents.

Over 800 pages with 1500 photos and illustrations with more than 30 video links taken by the author in his adventurous travels. This series also comes with a **Teachers' Guide** and **Student Practical Manual.**

This large (A4 sized) textbook has been broken up into a series of eight small-sized books for easier reading by everyone age 12+. The series includes:

Exploration Science. Field Geology and Mapping

Riches from the Earth. Minerals, Energy and Mining

A Dangerous Planet. Volcanoes and Earthquakes

Changing the Surface. Erosion and Landscapes

Rocks- Building the Earth. Rocks and their formation

Fossils -Life in the Rocks. Studying ancient life and its environment

Through Sea and Sky. Oceanography and Meteorology

Beyond Planet Earth, an Introduction to Astronomy. A complete guide to studying the universe.

Adventures in Earth and Environmental Science Series

Adventures in Earth and Environmental Science Series – Books 1 and 2. A two volume extension of the previous series with emphasis on the environment both in climate and on the surface and is based on the Australian national syllabus in Environmental Science. Each volume comes with a **Student Practical Manual** and there is also a **Teachers' Guide**.